Gaines, Ernest J HB
In my father's house.

ALSO BY ERNEST J. GAINES

Catherine Carmier

Of Love and Dust

Bloodline

The Autobiography of Miss Jane Pittman

A Long Day in November (for children)

In My Father's House

In My Father's House

ERNEST J. GAINES

ALFRED A. KNOPF NEW YORK 1978

THIS IS A BORZOI BOOK PUBLISHED BY ALFRED A. KNOPF, INC.

 Published in the United States by Alfred A. Knopf, Inc., New York, and simultaneously in Canada by Random House of Canada Limited, Toronto. Distributed by Random House, Inc., New York.

Library of Congress Cataloging in Publication Data
Gaines, Ernest J. [date]
In my father's house.
I. Title.
PZ4.G1422In [PS3557.A355] 813'.5'4 77-20357
ISBN 0-394-47938-6

Manufactured in the United States of America
Published May 25, 1978
Second Printing Before Publication

To the memory of George and Mamie Williams
and Octavia McVay—
They gave you whatever they had; they asked
you for nothing in return

In My Father's House

1

Virginia Colar was standing in the kitchen looking out of the window at the rain when she heard the knocking at the front door. She could see how the wind was blowing the limbs in the pecan tree, and she thought the knocking was no more than a limb brushing against the sides of the house. She turned from the window to check the pot of soup that she had cooking on the stove. After tasting it to see if it was seasoned well enough, she nodded her head with satisfaction and lowered the flame.

She heard the knocking again, this time louder than before. She was sure now that somebody was out there, and she went to the front to see who it was. When she opened the door she saw a thin, brown-skinned young man standing before her in a wet overcoat. Water dripped from his knitted Army field cap down his face, leaving crystal drops hanging from the scraggly beard on his chin.

"You got rooms?" he asked her.

"I got—" But she cut it off.

She didn't like his looks. He was too thin, too hungry-looking. She didn't like the little twisted knots of hair on his face that passed for a beard. He looked sick. His jaws were too sunken-in for someone his age. His deep-set bloodshot eyes wandered too much. He could have just been released from the state pen. He definitely looked like somebody who had been shut in. They probably had let him go because they figured they had punished him enough already and knew he would die soon.

Something in the back of her mind told her to tell him that she had made a mistake about having rooms. She had just rented the last one to a— an insurance man that very morning. But she asked herself where else would he go? Uptown to one of those back rooms of that white motel? Would they let him in there? By law they were supposed to, but couldn't they say they didn't have any vacancy either?

After looking him over again, still telling herself that she would be doing the wrong thing, she moved to the side to let him come in. His only luggage was a half-full laundry bag slung over his right shoulder. After he had passed her she looked outside again. She was looking for Fletcher Zeno's cab. Fletcher was the only black cab driver in St. Adrienne, and he met every bus that came into the station. But Virginia knew before looking outside that the cab would not be there. The young man's clothes and the laundry bag would not have been so wet if Fletcher had brought him to the house.

"That's a dollar a day," she said, still holding the door open. She wished he would say a dollar was too much for a room, then she would have had a good excuse to send him back out there.

"I like it for a week," he said.

"Seven dollars," she said. "And I 'preciates my money in advance."

She waited until he had reached toward his pocket before she closed the door and told him to follow her to her office. Her office was a small desk and a chair that she had sitting in one corner of her living room. At the door she told him to stay out in the hall, while she went into the room to get his key and the receipt book.

"Where you from?" she called from inside.

He didn't answer her.

She came back out.

"I asked where you was from?" she demanded this time.

Virginia was short, stocky, and very black. Her hair, which had only recently been straightened, was no more than a couple of inches long. Her face was round and oilish. Because she was so much shorter than the young man she was talking to, she had to throw her head back to look him in the face. She looked at him as fiercely as she could. She wanted him to know she expected an answer when she spoke, and she wanted him to know that she was doing him a favor by taking him in on a day like this.

"Chicago," he told her.

She looked at him a moment longer, then she looked at the blue laundry bag that he still had slung over his shoulder. She didn't believe he was from Chicago.

"Money," she said, reaching out her hand.

He gave her a wrinkled five-dollar bill and some change. The change money was black with age, as though it had not been used in a long time.

"Your name?" she asked him.

"Robert," he said.

"Last name?"

"X."

Virginia was holding the receipt book against the wall while she wrote down the information. When she heard him say "X" she drew down one line and stopped. She wasn't looking at him yet; she was still looking at the receipt book, trying to recall what group of people called themselves "X." She couldn't remember now whether it was the Black Panthers or the Black Muslims.

Something in the back of her mind told her to give him

back his money. But something else said, Where else would he go? Uptown? The whites wouldn't let him in there either. They had turned down fatter ones and drier ones than he. And she was sure no "X" had ever slept in any one of those beds.

She turned to him. "I don't want no trouble in here," she said. "I run a nice orderly place here. I don't bother the law, the law doesn't bother me. You hear me, don't you?"

He didn't answer her, he wasn't even looking at her, he was looking at the receipt book that she held against the wall. She had drawn half of his last name, and he might have been looking at that. But Virginia couldn't tell from his gaze where his mind was. She slashed the other line across the first and told him to follow her upstairs.

"You musta walked from the station?" she said.

When he didn't answer her, she waited until she had climbed another step before she stopped and looked back at him. He was standing two steps below her. Beads of water still clung to his beard, and that blue laundry bag was slung over his shoulders as if he was leaving instead of coming in.

"I'm 'customed to people answering me," she said.

"I walked," he said.

"Wasn't Fletcher there?" she asked. "A little ugly black man with red, beady—"

"He was."

"Was?" she said. She wanted to say: "And he didn't stick a gun in your back?" or "And he didn't drag you to his cab?" But she didn't say either, because he wouldn't even have heard her. Something in the back of her mind told her again to give him back his seven dollars. But something else asked her, Where else would he go?

She led him up to his room and lit the little gas heater, then she went to the bathroom down the hall to get a bucket of water to set on top of the heater. The water would keep moisture in the room. All the time that she was in the room with him, he stood by the window looking out at the rain.

He hadn't taken the laundry bag from his shoulder or taken off the cap or unbuttoned the coat.

"The toilet and the shower down the hall there," she said, to his back. "I change sheets and pillow cases once a week—Saturday. These already clean, so I won't be changing them tomorrow. When you get hungry, the best place round here is Thelma's café—about three blocks farther back of town. Her husband, Wrigley, runs that nightclub next to it—place called the Congo Room—you can't miss it."

She could see he wasn't interested in what she was saying, and she went back downstairs to the kitchen. She dished up a bowl of soup and sat down at the table to eat. But she had eaten no more than a couple of spoonfuls when she thought about Fletcher, and she went up the hall to her office to telephone him. Fletcher's cab stand was at Thelma's café, and Fletcher must have been sitting at the counter or standing nearby, because as soon as Thelma answered the telephone, Virginia heard her say: "For you, Fletcher."

"Fletcher," he said.

"You rich, hanh?" Virginia asked him.

"I see," Fletcher said. "He found his way."

"So y'all did talk?" Virginia said. "And you didn't stick a gun in his back to make him get in that cab?"

"No, I didn't pull my gun this time," Fletcher said. "I just begged him. But begging don't work."

Virginia heard him drink something quickly. It could have been a cocktail he had gotten from the bar side, or a cup of hot coffee that he was drinking at the counter.

"You got your money?" he asked her. "He wasn't exactly tipping everybody at that bus station."

"I got a week in advance," Virgina said.

"That cold rain can do that," Fletcher said. "Can make you change your view on life right away." Then he laughed, quick and short. "He say where he's coming from?" he asked Virginia.

"Chicago," she said.

"Where?" Fletcher asked her.

"That's what he told me."

"With nothing but that blue laundry bag?" Fletcher asked.

"He calls himself Robert X," Virginia said.

"One of them, hanh?" Fletcher said. "Well, you got something on your hands now, sister."

"What you mean?"

"You'll find out," Fletcher said, and laughed again.

Virginia hung up the telephone and went back into the kitchen. From the table she could see the rain touching lightly against the windowpanes. She could see the soft swaying of limbs in the pecan tree beside the house. There was not a pecan on the tree, not even a single leaf; not one bird sat on any of the limbs. The tree, bare, gray, was the same color as the low-hanging sky above it.

I don't like the look of this weather, I don't like the feel of it, Virginia thought to herself. Trouble always 'company weather like this.

She thought about her tenant upstairs in number four, and she wondered if he was hungry. She didn't serve food at the house, but she had cooked much more than she would ever eat. If she ate soup every day for a week, there would still be some left over.

It was her conscience bothering her again, she told herself. It wasn't satisfied that it had made her let him into the house, but now it was trying to make her feed him too.

After she had finished eating, she dished up another bowl of soup, and with some crackers on a plate, she took the food up to his room. She knocked twice, and when he didn't answer her, she opened the door and went in. She would set the plate on the bucket of water, and the food would still be warm when he woke up. She was halfway across the room when she suddenly felt as though she was being watched, and she jerked her head round to face the bed. He was not watching her, but he was lying there wide awake. The wet overcoat and the knitted Army cap hung on a nail against the wall, both smoking from the heat in the room. For a moment Virginia was too angry to do anything but stare down at him. She couldn't make up her mind whether to curse him and leave the food or curse him and take it back to the kitchen.

"You bastard," she said. "You bastard."

Without answering her, he pushed himself up on the bed and reached into his pocket to get her some money.

"It's free," she said. "I don't serve no food here. And I don't take too much nonsense either. I hope you remember that."

She set the plate on the small lamp table at the head of the bed and backed away from him. She had reached the door when she heard him asking: "Any churches back here?"

Virginia considered herself a Christian above anything else. A moment ago she cursed her tenant, but hearing him ask about church, she was ready to forgive him.

"Churches?" she said. "We got three—if you said churches?"

He picked up his plate and started eating. He nodded his head without looking round at her.

"You need to go to church?" she asked, hoping that he would say yes.

"No," he said.

"You just want to know where they at?"

He didn't even nod his head this time.

"We have two Baptist and a Catholic," she said. "But we don't have none for the Mus—" She cut it off.

"Baptist," she heard him say.

"We got a Baptist church just up the street there," she told him. "Solid Rock Baptist Church. My church. Reverend Phillip J. Martin, pastor. Maybe you done heard of Reverend Martin up there in Chicago?"

He went on eating, without answering her. She figured he didn't know about the minister.

"He's our civil rights leader round here," she said. "Everybody round here proud of him. Done such a good job here, people thinking 'bout sending him on to Washington. Would be the first one from round here, you know."

"Must be a good man," Virginia heard him say.

"The people here think so," she told him. " 'Course you have some 'gainst him—white and black. You go'n find that no matter where you go. But most of the people all for him. He'll be a good man in Washington. Sure done some wonderful things here for us."

"What's he done?" the tenant asked without looking round.

"What's he done?" Virginia said. "What's he done?" She didn't mind his being ignorant of her pastor's work, but it sounded from the tone of his voice that he didn't believe what she was saying. "He's done everything," she said. "Everything. That's what he's done—everything. Changed just about everything round here, 'cept for old Chenal up there. But it won't be long 'fore Chenal fall too. He'll fall just like all the rest. Old white man we got uptown don't want pay the colored nothing for working. Own the biggest store up there, everybody go in his store, still don't want pay nobody nothing for working. He'll change his tune when Phillip get through with him—you mark my word."

The tenant went on eating his food as if he were in the room alone. Virginia felt that she would have been talking only to the walls if she had stood there any longer.

That evening, just after dark, he came downstairs and left the house. Virginia stayed up watching television late, but never heard him come back in. The next morning around six o'clock, even before she had gotten out of bed, the cab driver, Fletcher Zeno, called her on the telephone.

"Want hear something good?" he asked her.

"No," she said, and hung up.

The telephone rang again.

"What you want, Fletcher?" she said. "You know what time it is?"

"Five minutes to six, 'cording to my old Waterbury," Fletcher said. Virginia heard him drink something quickly. She figured he was at home and was drinking hot coffee. "Seen your boy sitting behind Reverend Martin's church door last night," he said. "Round midnight, on my way home. First, I took him for a ghost. Then I thought it might be a dog. I went up to Brick O'Linde's and turned round and came on back. I still couldn't make out what it was, all slumped down like that, so I got out the car. Maybe it was Unc Matty or Dago Jack sick there and couldn't make it home. But halfway up the walk I seen who it was—your boy there. Slumped back 'gainst that door with his hands jabbed down in his pockets. Coulda been 'sleep for all I know. I turned around and went on home. Well?" Another sip from his hot coffee. "What you think? Think he's crazy—or just like cold rain?"

"I don't think he's crazy, I don't think he likes cold rain neither," Virgina said. "I think you making all that up 'cause you didn't get that seventy-five cents yesterday."

Fletcher told that same story to others that day, and like Virginia not many wanted to believe him. Two days later everyone did. Monday at Thelma's café, Abe Matthews told the people how he had seen Virginia's new tenant standing under one of the big oak trees in the cemetery. He had seen him there on Sunday evening just as it was getting dark, so he was not ready to swear on the Bible that it was the tenant, but if it wasn't, then it was a ghost wearing a long overcoat and a knitted cap pulled all the way down to his ears. Evalena Battley, on her way to work at the St. Adrienne laundry, saw him at six o'clock in the morning standing on the bank of the St. Charles River. The rain had been falling steadily the past two weeks, and now the river was high and rough, flowing swiftly south toward New Orleans. The tenant stood on the bank among the hanging branches of the weeping willow, oblivious to Evalena, to everything else round him except the swift-flowing river.

That same evening, Dago Jack, on his way home from Brick O'Linde's grocery store, saw him standing out in the street watching Phillip Martin's house. Dago mentioned it to the people at the store the next day, but since they had seen him practically everywhere else already they didn't think much of it.

He had two meals at Thelma's café. On Saturday, the day after he arrived in St. Adrienne, he came into the café around noon and sat down at a table in the corner. When Thelma told him what she had on the menu for the day, he told her to bring him a plate of red beans and rice, mustard greens, and a piece of cornbread. The next day he came back about the same time, and he ordered giblets, rice, greens, and cornbread. He sat at the same table as before, a little red-and-white-checkered, oilcloth-covered table in the corner. Neither time did he take off his cap or his coat. Both times he paid for his meals with change money. The money, quarters, nickels, dimes, was black with age.

Monday he started buying his food at Brick O'Linde's grocery store. Several men, including the cab driver Fletcher Zeno, sat or stood round the heater talking. They had been talking about him just before he came in, but now they were quiet, one then another glancing at him standing at the counter. He bought sausage, cheese, bread, and a bottle of cheap muscatel wine. After he had paid for his groceries he left the store without saying a word to anyone.

"More of that black money?" Fletcher asked Brick.

Brick O'Linde looked at the money in the palm of his hand and nodded his head.

That evening they saw him walking again. He never

spoke to anyone. He never asked anyone about anyone else. Yet, day and night, whether it was raining or not, they would meet him or pass him walking the street. Several people had seen him on St. Anne Street, not far from the house where the minister and civil rights leader Phillip Martin lived.

2

Elijah Green, a teacher at the elementary school in St. Adrienne, lived with Phillip Martin and his family. He gave piano lessons to the minister's ten-year-old daughter, Joyce Anne, as payment for his room and board. He was also choir director at the church and worked in the civil rights program. He gave regular parties at the house for the workers and their supporters, and the next one would be held that coming Saturday.

Thursday evening, two days before the party, he was driving up St. Anne Street when the lights of his car flashed on Virginia's new tenant walking up ahead of him. He recognized the overcoat from a block away. He had seen him several times before, but like everyone else he had been apprehensive about approaching him. He told himself that this time he would. He stopped just ahead of the tenant and leaned over to the passenger door to speak to him.

"Give you a lift?" he asked.

The tenant stuck his narrow, beaded face into the window, then straightened up to look back down the street. Elijah couldn't see his face now, so he couldn't tell what he was looking at or looking for. But the next moment he had opened the door and gotten in. Elijah smiled timidly as he reached out his hand. Their hands were opposites. The tenant's fingers were long and skeletal, the knuckles as prominent as knots on a stick. Elijah, who was short and very dark, had small, soft hands.

"You going far?" he asked, after driving off.

"Just walking," the tenant said, as if he knew that Elijah had picked him up only to ask him questions.

"Walk a lot, huh?" Elijah asked.

The tenant looked at him and nodded his head. "I walk a lot," he said.

"Pretty bad weather to be walking in," Elijah said, after glancing out of the window up at the sky. "Been like this now couple of weeks."

"I don't mind the weather," the tenant said. "You mind the weather?"

Elijah grinned to himself. "Don't reckon you can do much about it," he said. "But I rather have it warm and sunny."

"For what?" the tenant asked him.

"It just feels better," Elijah answered.

"It all feels the same to me," the tenant said.

Elijah looked at the scraggly, bearded face. The tenant was gazing out in front of the car. Elijah couldn't think of anything else to say.

"Your house back there?" the tenant asked, after they had been silent a while.

Elijah realized now why he had looked back just before getting into the car. He had seen a car parked before the minister's house, and he had to be sure that this was the same one.

"What house?" Elijah asked, as if he didn't know what the tenant was talking about.

"The brick house," he said without looking at Elijah.

"No, I just have a room there," Elijah said. "That's Reverend Martin's house."

"Reverend Martin?" the tenant asked, still not looking at Elijah.

"Our civil rights leader round here," Elijah said. "Our Martin Luther King, you might say."

"That's pretty high class," the tenant said.

"We feel he's in that class," Elijah told him.

"How do you come to that?" the tenant asked.

"By his work," Elijah said. "His leadership, political and moral. His character."

"His character?" the tenant asked. "Do you ever know a man's character?"

"I think I know his," Elijah said. "I've known him ten years. Been living with them five years. I think I know something about him."

The tenant grunted and nodded his head as he gazed out at the light in front of the car.

"Heard you were from Chicago?" Elijah asked him. "Visiting some people here in St. Adrienne?"

Elijah knew better. Like everyone else in St. Adrienne who had seen Virginia's new tenant walking the streets, he knew that he had not visited anyone. But Elijah wanted to hear how he would answer.

"I'm here for a conference," he said.

"What kind of conference?"

"A black man's conference."

"Here in St. Adrienne?"

"I'm meeting a man here in St. Adrienne."

"Does he live here? Do we know him?"

The tenant didn't answer him, and Elijah thought it was best not to ask any more questions for a while. He turned off St. Anne Street, which was very wide and well-lighted, onto a narrow dark street with ditches on either side. Weathered-gray shotgun houses, their doors shut tight against the cold, sat only a few feet from the ditches. Hardly any light could be seen anywhere on the street or from the houses.

"Going to be here long?" Elijah asked, after they had gone a couple more blocks.

"It depends," the tenant said.

"We're having a little party at the house Saturday evening," Elijah told him. "Drop by if you're still around."

His passenger turned quickly to look at him. For the first time since getting into the car he seemed very interested in what Elijah was saying.

"You mean that brick house back there?" he asked.

Elijah nodded. "Yes, Reverend Martin's house."

The tenant smiled from the side of his mouth and narrowed his eyes as he looked down at Elijah. "You don't think he'd mind, somebody like me coming in his house?"

"Mind?" Elijah asked.

The tenant nodded his head. "Mind."

"Mind for what?" Elijah asked him. "That's why we're giving the party, so people can come there."

"Even people like me?" the tenant said, and touched his chest.

"Anybody and everybody," Elijah said. Then he looked up at him. "Long as you don't bite people. You don't bite people, do you?"

The tenant shook his head. "No, I don't bite people."

Elijah grinned at him. "Then you welcomed," he said.

Up ahead of them, Elijah could see the green-and-yellow neon lights flashing over the door of the Congo Room. He could tell by the cars parked before the door and to the side that the other teachers were already at the bar.

"Care to have a drink?" he asked his passenger.

"No, thanks."

"Can I drop you off anywhere?"

"No, I'll walk."

Elijah stopped before the Congo Room, but his passenger did not get out of the car. He sat very erect, looking at the lights flashing over the door. Elijah figured he was sitting there because he had no place to go, other than back to that room or to walk the streets.

"Sure you won't have that drink?" he asked him again.

"No. I'll see you Saturday," the tenant said, and got out.

After shutting the door, he nodded back to Elijah through the glass.

"I'll have one of my friends pick you up," Elijah said.

"I'll be there," he answered, and walked away.

Elijah sat watching him go up the street, until the coat became the same color as the darkness, then he got out of the car and went into the bar. He had no sooner stepped inside when he heard someone call his name, and he pushed his way through the crowd over to the table where the other teachers were sitting. There were about a half dozen men and women at the table. They were in their twenties or early thirties, and they taught at either the elementary school or the junior high school in St. Adrienne. They came into the Congo Room every evening to drink and talk. It was the best nightclub in St. Adrienne for blacks and the only one where the teachers would go.

"What kept you so long?" a man wearing a plaid sport jacket asked Elijah. "The bottle's almost gone."

On the table was about a quarter of a fifth of whiskey, a half pitcher of water, a couple of bottles of soft drinks, and a plastic bowl of ice cubes. Elijah fixed himself a drink and sat down.

"I met Virginia's new tenant, Robert X," he said.

"You walking too?" the young man in the sport jacket asked, and laughed. His name was Chuck Allen.

"I gave him a lift," Elijah said. "Tried to get him to come in and have a drink, but he had somewhere to go."

"Maybe he had to get in some more walking," Chuck Allen said, and laughed again.

"He's here for a conference," Elijah said.

"Here in St. Adrienne?" Chuck asked. "What kind of conference?"

"Some kind of black man's conference," Elijah said. "He's here to meet somebody. I suppose the conference is somewhere else."

"Here to meet who?" Chuck asked.

"He didn't say," Elijah said, and drank.

"If the other person walk much as he does, maybe they'll bump into each other," a light-skinned man named Guy Christophe said from the other end of the table.

"Niggers have more conferences than the President," Chuck said, after drinking. "But you never hear of a damned thing come out of them."

"One thing always come out of them," Christophe said. "They always make plans for the next conference."

Several of the other teachers laughed.

"I invited him to the party, Shep," Elijah said to the teacher sitting directly across from him.

Shepherd Lewis, wearing a green cardigan over a brown open-collar shirt, sat at the table with a hand on his glass and the other arm on the back of the chair of the woman sitting next to him. He looked across the table at Elijah and frowned. He knew Elijah had some plan for him.

"Your party," he said. "Invite who you want."

"I would like for you to bring him when you come," Elijah said.

"Well, I'll be damned," Shepherd said.

"I'll probably be busy all day," Elijah said. "I told him one of my friends would bring him over."

"Your friend didn't pick him up," Shepherd said.

"I didn't think you'd mind," Elijah said, apologizing.

"I do mind," Shepherd said.

"Don't worry, Elijah, he'll bring him over," the woman sitting next to Shepherd said.

"Will I?" he asked her.

"Sure," she said, looking up at him.

Her name was Beverly Ricord. She had very light skin, and her long brown hair was twisted and pinned into a bun on the back of her head. She and Shepherd had been lovers ever since their days at Southern University in Baton Rouge where he was a football hero. He was a handsome fellow, and there were many girls, but he loved her most. After graduating from the university he tried out for professional football, but he couldn't make it and he got a job teaching at the same school where she was. They had been working together now over seven years, and she had been trying to get him to marry her ever since.

"About time you did something nice for somebody," she said.

"I'm not nice, huh?" he asked, looking down at her.

"Sometimes. Sometimes no," she said, and fixed her own drink. She drank and looked at him. "Sometimes no."

Shepherd turned to Elijah, but Elijah had discreetly looked away. No one else at the table said anything for a while.

"What you go'n have at your party to drink, Elijah?" Chuck asked.

"Eggnog. Punch," Elijah said. He didn't look at Chuck, because he would have to look past Shepherd to do so.

"Anything in that eggnog and punch?" Chuck asked.

Elijah shook his head. "No."

"Well, don't expect to see me," Chuck said.

"And ditto for me," Christophe said from the other end of the table.

"That whole thing's over with," Chuck said, after he had fixed himself another drink. "He did some good work, but it's all over with now. What you say, Shep?"

Shepherd shook his head. "I don't know," he said. He was still mad at Elijah, and he didn't feel like talking.

"The man's beautiful, so much courage," Beverly said.

"I wish I had courage like that. I'd give anything to have courage like that."

"Well," Chuck said, raising his glass. "Here's to good old courage. All the luck in the world to good old courage."

"I think it's a shame," Beverly said. "We being the teachers, we ought to be the ones out there in front."

"Well, you can represent me, baby," Chuck said. He turned and raised his hand so the bartender would notice him and bring another bottle. The bartender nodded his head. Chuck looked back at Beverly. "That shit's over with, kiddo. Them honkies gave up some, because of conscience, because of God. But they ain't giving up no more. Nigger's already got just about everything he's getting out of this little town. Anything else he want he better go look somewhere else for it."

The bartender brought the bottle.

3

After Virginia's new tenant left Elijah Thursday evening, no one saw him again until Shepherd went to the house Saturday to bring him to the party. Why he had suddenly stopped walking the streets no one knew. But now he stayed in his room. The people on either side of him could hear him pacing the floor day and night. Friday night, sometime between twelve and one o'clock, they heard him scream. Virginia heard it too and ran out into the hall. Someone told her where the noise had come from, and she went upstairs and knocked on his door. He didn't answer. She knocked again and put her ear to the door this time. She could hear him crying quietly, as though he might be lying on the bed with his face in the covers. She knocked and listened. She told one of the men to knock. The man knocked very hard with his fist. Then both he and Virginia put their ears to the door. But now even the crying had stopped.

Virginia didn't get any sleep the rest of the night, and all day Saturday she was nervous and tense. When she was under stress, she either cooked food all day or spent the day fixing her hair. That day she did both. When Shepherd came up to the house she had straightened her hair, but she hadn't finished curling it. There were curls only on one side; the other side looked like so many porcupine quills. Shepherd would have laughed at her, but he could see she was scared.

"Something the matter?" he asked her.

"I don't know," she said, looking up at him and shaking her head. "I don't know."

Shepherd was a little over six feet tall, and Virginia threw her head back to look up at him. Her round black face was shining from the hot comb that she had put down only a moment ago.

"He pushed some money under my door for another week, but I don't know," she said, looking up at Shepherd.

"I guess he's still waiting for that other person—his friend—to show up," Shepherd said.

"What friend?" Virginia said. "He ain't got no friend. He ain't got nobody. And he ain't going to no conference neither. I know it, you know it, and everybody else round here know it."

"All I know, Elijah invited him to the party, and he wants me to bring him there," Shepherd said.

"That poor little sissy," Virginia said. "What's he want get messed up with this thing for?"

Shepherd grinned at Virginia's description of Elijah. "You know Elijah," he said. "He feels sorry for everything. Then he let somebody else do the work."

"Well, I can't say nothing 'bout Elijah," Virginia said. "Didn't he get in here? And ain't I done even fed him? And how many times I done burnt myself today? I take that top off the pot, with no dishrag. I put that comb so close to my scalp you can hear it frying clear to Brick O'Linde. All 'cause of him. Screaming and going on."

"Screaming?" Shepherd asked her.

"Last night there after midnight. Nearly scared me to death. I ran up there and knocked on the door, but you think he'd answer? Abe Matthews almost knocked the door down with his fist—you think he'd answer? God knows I don't know what I got myself into."

"Look what I got myself into," Shepherd said. "I have to escort him to a party."

"You, you can get out of it," Virginia said. "Just go back and tell Elijah you couldn't find him. Tell him he went walking somewhere and you don't know where he's at."

"Beverly wants me to bring him to the party, too," Shepherd said. "That's why I'm here. She wants me to be nice to people. I'm not nice enough, she said."

"How is Beverly?" Virginia asked. She had forgotten about her tenant for a moment.

"She's all right," Shepherd said.

"When y'all getting married, Shepherd?" Virginia asked seriously.

"It never crossed my mind," he said.

"You ought to marry her, Shepherd," Virginia told him. "She's a nice girl, even if she is Catholic and Creole. It be good for both of y'all. Keep both of you out of them bars, for one thing."

Shepherd didn't want to talk about his personal life. "What room is he in?" he asked Virginia.

"Four," Virginia said.

Both of them turned and looked toward the stairs.

"Something's wrong up there," Virginia said. Now she had forgotten about Beverly, and she was thinking about her tenant again. "I can't put my finger on it, but something's wrong up there. How I got in it, only God knows."

Shepherd went upstairs and knocked on the door. He had to knock a second time before the door opened. The new tenant stood before him in a wrinkled brown shirt and wrinkled brown slacks, his hair uncombed, his eyes bloodshot and weak as if he had not slept for days. This was the first time Shepherd had seen him up close, and for a moment he could do nothing but stare at him. The tenant waited to hear what he had to say.

"Elijah sent me," he said finally. "To bring you to the party."

"What party?"

"At Reverend Martin's house," Shepherd told him.

"What day is it?"

"Saturday."

He turned and went back inside, sitting down on the bed facing the window. Shepherd stood at the door a moment, then followed him into the room. The room stank with the odor of cheap wine. Now Shepherd wished he had stayed out in the hall.

"You want me to come back later?" he asked.

The tenant didn't answer him. Instead, he reached for the bottle of wine on the lamp table. He drank about half of what was left in the bottle and set the bottle back.

"That stuff's no good," Shepherd said.

"It kills the pain," the tenant answered quietly.

"You had anything to eat?"

"A sandwich."

"When?" Shepherd asked.

"I don't know," the tenant answered.

Shepherd had come closer to the bed and he could see all the wrapping papers on the floor against the wall. About a half dozen wine bottles were on the floor with the paper. It seemed that nothing had been thrown out since Virginia's new tenant had started buying his food at the grocery store. The covers and the sheets on the bed were rumpled and pushed to one side. The bed probably had not been made up either since he had been sleeping in it.

The tenant got up from the bed and went to the window. Shepherd stood back a moment, then followed him.

"My soul don't feel good," he said as he stared down at the alley that ran alongside the building. "Like garbage, broke glass, tin cans. Any trash."

"Can I do something?" Shepherd asked him.

He shook his head without looking round. "Nobody can do nothing," he said.

"Maybe you ought to see a doctor."

"A doctor can't do me no good."

"Why don't you go back home?" Shepherd said with sympathy.

The tenant grunted quietly to himself. "Home?"

"Don't you have a home?"

He nodded his head, as he continued to stare down into the alley below the window.

"I had a home once," he said.

"Where did you come from?"

"A prison."

"You're just getting out of prison?"

"You can call it that."

For a moment Shepherd watched him without saying anything else. He seemed unaware of Shepherd even being in the room. The room was small, gray; the furniture old and worn. His coat and cap hung on a nail against the wall. Shepherd had looked round at the things in the room, and now he looked back at the tenant again.

"Why don't you change," he told him. "We ought to get moving."

"Everything is like this," the tenant said without looking round.

"Do you have another shirt?"

"Just like this one," the tenant said. "It's blue, not brown."

"We can drop by my place and pick up something," Shepherd said. He didn't like the idea of sharing his clothes with this fellow, but he would do anything to get out of the room.

The tenant didn't seem to be listening to him. His whole interest was directed toward the alley below the window. The alley was strewn with broken bottles, rusty tin cans, bits of paper, and any other kind of debris imaginable.

"Is that how life is?" he asked, still not looking round. "Like that alley down there?"

Shepherd looked down at the trash below the window.

"Used to be something good in them bottles, in them cans," the tenant said. "Somebody went through lot of pain making them bottles round—red and green. Look at them now. Busted. Cans bent and rusted. Nothing but trash. Nothing but trash now."

"Life's not like that," Shepherd said. "Man's not made of glass and tin."

"It all adds up to the same thing," the tenant said. "No matter what you do, no matter how hard you work, how much you love, they catch you off guard one day and break you. It don't matter if you're glass and tin, or meat and bone. It don't matter." He turned to Shepherd. "Why don't you go on," he said. "I can see him some other time."

"Elijah told me to bring you," Shepherd said. "My old lady told me not to show up without you."

"Why?" he asked.

"She says I'm not nice enough to people."

"You're nice," the tenant said.

"Not according to her. Not often enough."

"I don't want to be no burden on you," the tenant said.

"You won't be a burden."

"That's cause you don't know me," he said. "If you knowed me, I'd be a burden."

"Know you how?" Shepherd asked him.

"I'm go'n die soon," the tenant said, looking sadly at Shepherd.

"Are you sick?" Shepherd asked him.

"I'm sick," the tenant said calmly. "My soul is sick. My soul."

"Then you need to see a priest, or a preacher, or somebody like that," Shepherd said.

The tenant suddenly laughed in Shepherd's face. Shepherd didn't know what he had said that was so funny, but he laughed too. The tenant turned from him and looked down into the alley again.

"Come on," Shepherd said.

"I'm not a freak," the tenant said.

"Nobody's calling you a freak," Shepherd said. "All right, I'll go and tell them you didn't want to come. If you change your mind, call the house."

He turned away from him and started out of the room. He was near the door when the tenant said, "Wait." Shepherd stopped and looked back at him, but the tenant still looked down into the alley.

"Yes?" Shepherd said.

The tenant turned from the window and picked up the bottle from the lamp table.

"I wouldn't drink that stuff," Shepherd said.

He drank it all and set the bottle back on the table.

"When I'm gone, you'll know why I had to drink it," he said.

He got his overcoat and knitted cap from against the wall and followed Shepherd out of the room.

The minister lived about a quarter of a mile farther back of town. His ranch-style brick house was the most expensive and elegant owned by a black family in St. Adrienne. The house sat behind a thick green lawn of St. Augustine grass about fifty feet away from the road. A driveway covered with sea shells ran along the right side of the yard, ending under a canopy beside the house. The minister's big Chrysler and his wife's smaller station wagon were parked there. Other cars were on the drive and before the door. Shepherd parked half a block down the street, and he and the new tenant walked back to the house.

The big living room, with a fire in the fireplace, was crowded and noisy. The people were all well-dressed, and most of them were older than Shepherd and the new tenant. Two years earlier half of the crowd would have been their ages, but with Martin Luther King's death many of the younger people had left the program.

Shepherd and the new tenant had been in the room only a little while when Shepherd noticed the minister's wife coming toward them. Alma Martin, a small brown-skinned woman, wore a long dark-green dress with a black patent-leather belt round the waist. She was only thirty-five years old, but her calm, passive face and dark clothes made her look much older. She spoke so quietly when she asked for their coats that they could hardly hear her over the noise in the room. Shepherd had taken off his hat and coat when he came inside, but the tenant kept his on.

Shepherd introduced them. The tenant nodded politely, looked at her for only a second, and looked away. Alma wasn't surprised. Most people usually ignored her and worshipped her husband. After telling them she wished they would have a good time at the party she left with Shepherd's hat and overcoat. Halfway cross the room she met Elijah, who had just come in with a tray of cups and glasses. Shepherd could see them talking, and a moment later Elijah was coming toward them.

"What a madhouse," he said. "What a madhouse. Everybody showed up. I'm running all over the place. Good Lord, Robert, but aren't you burning up in that coat?"

"He wants to keep it on," Shepherd said. "What you got in them cups, eggnog?"

"Yes."

"Anything else?"

"Plain eggnog."

Shepherd and the new tenant both took a cup off the tray.

"Beverly showed up yet?" Shepherd asked Elijah.

"I thought she was coming with you," Elijah said.

"She had to go on the Island," Shepherd said. "I thought she'd be back by now."

Elijah turned from Shepherd to the new tenant. "Well, Robert X, how've you been? Haven't seen you since Thursday evening. Thought maybe you had left us already. I suppose your friend hasn't showed up yet, huh?"

The tenant shook his head but did not answer. He had

been looking round the room as if he was looking for someone.

"Shepherd, I'm going to be a little busy for a while," Elijah said. "You don't mind showing Robert X around, do you?"

Shepherd did mind; he thought he had already done enough. But before he could say anything, Elijah had turned from them and he was pushing his way through the crowd again.

"Want to move around?" Shepherd asked the tenant.

"I'm good here."

Shepherd didn't want to move either. He expected Beverly any moment, and he wanted to stay near the door to see her when she came in. He drank from his cup of eggnog while looking the people over in the room. Then finding the minister, he nodded his head and waved his cup in that direction.

"Over there by the piano," he said to the tenant. "Big man in the dark suit, talking to the white folks. King Martin himself."

Shepherd was still looking at Phillip Martin and not at the tenant, so he didn't see how violently the tenant's face trembled when he saw the minister for the first time. The tenant raised the cup to his mouth to calm himself and held it there with both hands. Shepherd didn't look round at him for a moment, and when he did he saw him staring across the room like someone hypnotized. His face was covered with sweat.

"What's the matter?" Shepherd asked him. "Something the matter?"

The tenant didn't answer. He seemed not even to hear Shepherd and stared across the room as though in a trance. Shepherd grabbed the sleeve of his coat and jerked at him.

"What's the matter with you?" he whispered.

The tenant snapped his head back and looked at Shepherd as if Shepherd had just woken him up. Then he pulled his arm free and wiped the sweat from his face.

"I'm all right," he said.

"Why don't you get out of that coat?" Shepherd told him. "You want to step outside for some fresh air?"

He shook his head. "No, I'm all right."

"You sure you're all right?"

"I'm all right."

He had been breathing quick and hard. Now he took in a deep breath and exhaled loudly as he looked down at the floor.

Several other people who had seen what happened moved away from them, but a tall gray-headed man named Howard Mills came over to where they were. Mills had been watching them ever since they came into the room. He thought there was something familiar about Virginia's new tenant. Either he had seen him somewhere else before or he knew some of his people.

"Is he all right?" he asked Shepherd.

"I think so," Shepherd said.

Shepherd introduced them. Mills was the head deacon in Phillip Martin's church.

"Hear you from Chicago?" he said, after they shook hands. "Folks out this way?"

"No," the new tenant said, avoiding Mills's eyes.

"Ever been out this way before?" Mills asked him.

"No," he answered.

"New Orleans? Biloxi?" Mills asked.

"No."

"Look like I done seen you somewhere before," Mills said. "I ain't wrong 'bout faces too many times. Sure you ain't got no people this way? No aunts, no uncles, nobody like that?"

"I don't know nobody," he said.

Mills looked at him closely and grunted to himself. He

was still convinced that he knew him, or definitely knew some of his people. He turned to Shepherd.

"Well, Shepherd, how've you been?" he asked.

"Fine. And yourself, Deacon?" Shepherd said.

"Can't complain for an old man," Mills said. "We still hoping for some young blood in the program."

"I'm joining one day," Shepherd said.

"Sounds like something I heard before," Mills said and smiled at him.

While they stood there talking, the front door opened and Phillip's young assistant pastor came into the room. Jonathan Robillard looked the people over from the door, then seeing Howard Mills he came over to where he was. Robillard was just under six feet tall, brown-skinned, and very slender. His eyes—large, dark, and clear—seemed suspicious of everything round him. Mills introduced him to Virginia's new tenant. Jonathan nodded but didn't reach out his hand. The tenant seemed preoccupied anyhow.

"How are you, Shepherd?" Jonathan spoke.

"Okay, and you?"

"I see you found a little time to come on over, but I don't see any of your other school-teaching friends?"

"I suppose they're busy," Shepherd said.

"Sure," Jonathan said. "Sure. They're too busy. That's why we're in the shape we're in today, everybody's too busy." He turned from Shepherd to Mills. "I missed anything?" he asked him.

"He's still talking to Octave and Anthony," Mills said.

"I hope one day we won't have to depend on that crowd," Jonathan said.

"I hope one day be more of us walking together," Mills said.

"Yes, but not depend on them like he does," Jonathan said, looking cross the room at Phillip. "I don't mind advice. I don't mind participation, but I like to make up my own mind."

"He knows what he's doing," Mills said.

"I still believe *we* must bring our own together," Jonathan said. "Not them. We. We must do it."

"We can still use help," Mills said. "They in a position to help us. We ain't got no black attorney round here who can do what Anthony can do. And Octave's the only friend we have on the board of education. We need them, Jonathan."

"We still have to do it ourselves," Jonathan said. "Get what we can get from them, but don't trust them all the way. He trusts them too much. Mark my word, they'll let him down one day."

4

Elijah had put away his tray of cups and glasses, and now he stood in the center of the room clapping his hands for silence. The people were making too much noise to hear him, and he clapped again and stamped his foot. When everyone had quieted down, he told them that Reverend Martin wished to say a few words to them. The people turned to Phillip who was already surrounded by a small crowd.

Phillip Martin wore a black pinstriped suit, a light gray shirt, and a red polka-dot tie. He was sixty years old, just over six feet tall, and he weighed around two hundred pounds. His thick black hair and thick well-trimmed mustache were just beginning to show some gray. Phillip was a very handsome dark-brown-skinned man, admired by women, black and white. The black women spoke openly of their admiration for him, the white women said it around people they could trust. There were rumors that he was involved with women other than his wife, but whether these rumors were true or not he was very much respected by most of the people who knew him. And no one ever questioned his position as leader of the civil rights movement in the parish.

The people had begun to applaud Phillip, and he raised his hands for silence. Shepherd, who stood next to Virginia's new tenant in the back of the room, could see the two big rings on his fingers and the gold watch band round his wrist. The people would not stop applauding him, and Shepherd could see how the gold watch band sparkled in the light as Phillip shook his hands for silence.

Phillip told his audience that he didn't have a speech to give, that he only wanted to remind them about next Friday when the committee would meet with Albert Chenal.

"It took us years to get Mr. Chenal to hire black people in the first place," he said. "Now, after he hires them he don't want to pay them nothing. When we go up there Friday we go'n make it clear. Either he pay the black workers the same he pay the white, or we march before the door. Now, we spend more money in that store than white people do—the white people go to Baton Rouge and New Orleans—some of them even go up North and 'way to Europe. Poor black people don't have that kind of money to do all that traveling; we spend ours here in St. Adrienne. Therefore, we want our black workers to get the same pay, the same treatment, or we close down shop. We'll see how long he can last if no blacks go in his store. Mr. Chenal—"

Elijah standing in the center of the room led the applause. He clapped his hands over his head and turned completely around so others would see him and join him. Phillip waited until he had quiet again.

"But Mr. Chenal will challenge us," he went on. "Sure as I'm standing here talking to you, Mr. Chenal will challenge us. First, he'll offer us pennies. When we turn that down, he'll make it nickels. Turn that down, then dimes. When we turn all of this down, he go'n tell us to get out. See how long we can take the cold. You may recall he did the same thing before—not when it was cold, when it was hot. He beat us when it was hot. Yes, when it was hot. And you know how much black people love hot weather—we thrive on hot weather."

The people started laughing, and Phillip held up his hands.

"Just why d'you think so many our people leaving the North and coming back home?" he asked them. "Our good old Southern hot weather, that's why. Still, we let Mr. Chenal beat us on the hottest day. Took the crumbs he offered us and said thanks. So what will he do now, knowing how much black people hate cold weather? He go'n offer us crumbs again, and when we turn it down he go'n tell us to get out his store. In the back his mind he go'n be thinking, 'They can't take cold weather. Ten minutes out there with Mr. Jack Frost, they go'n run home and drink hot toddy. He-he-he.' Well, Mr. Chenal is wrong, deadly wrong, we can take cold weather." Phillip looked across the room. "What you say, Mills?"

Tall, gray-headed Howard Mills standing against the wall raised one big fist up in the air.

"Got my overcoat cleaned this week," he said. "And got me some new rubber boots to hit that rain."

The people laughed at Howard Mills.

"Jonathan, ain't you ready?" Phillip asked.

Jonathan, who stood next to Mills, raised both fists high up over his head.

"I'm ready to walk till next year this time," he said. "And I hope every last person in here is ready to do the same."

The people applauded Jonathan. Phillip waited for silence.

"Poor Albert Chenal," he said. "Poor, poor Albert Chenal. I don't hate Albert Chenal. I don't want you to hate Albert Chenal. I want you to pray for Albert Chenal. Tomorrow in church, pray for Albert Chenal. Before you go to bed tonight, pray for Albert Chenal. Remember, love thy neighbor as thyself."

One of the two white women in the room applauded quietly. But when no one else joined her in support of praying for Albert Chenal, she brought her applause to an abrupt end.

Phillip went on. "Love is the only thing. Understanding the only thing. Persistence, the only thing. Getting up tomorrow, trying again, the only thing. Keep on pushing, the only thing. You got some out there screaming Black Power. I say, what is Black Power but what we already doing and what we been trying to do all these years? Then you have that other crowd sitting in the bars—they even worse than the Black Power screamers—they saying, 'What's the use? Nothing will ever change. Hey, Mr. Wrigley, pour me another drink.' I'll call on Brother Mills again. What you say, Mills? You seen any changes round here?"

Mills nodded his gray head. "I'm a witness to it," he said.

"Jonathan?" Phillip said. "You been there too. Well?"

"I've seen progress," Jonathan said. "But we have a long way to go, a long way to go."

"Amen," Phillip said.

But Jonathan was not through. He raised both fists over his head and looked round at the people in the room. "We need more people," he said. "More young people. More old people. We need the ones in the bars. We need the schoolteachers. We need them who go to work for the white people every day of their lives. We need them all. All, all, all. No reason to stay back, no reason at all. The wall is crumbling—let's finish tearing it down."

"Amen, amen," Phillip said, as the people applauded Jonathan.

Jonathan wanted to say more, but Phillip didn't give him a chance to go on.

"I'll call on a sister now," Phillip said. "Remember our

sisters was out there first. Miss Daisy Bates, Miss Autherine Lucy, and countless more. And there's Sister Claiborne standing over there with her fine foxy self—you seen any changes, Sister Claiborne?"

A small gray-haired woman dressed entirely in black nodded her head to Phillip.

"Sister Jackson?" Phillip said. "Don't that bus run back of town now? And don't we even have a little bench there for you to sit on when you tired?"

Sister Jackson, who was about the same age as Sister Claiborne, also wearing black, and a red bouquet, nodded her head as Sister Claiborne had done.

"If you want to know about changes, talk to a couple of these sisters round here," Phillip went on. "Sister Aaron, can't you vote today for the mayor of St. Adrienne, the governor of Louisiana, the President of the United States?"

"Yes," Sister Aaron said. "And I'm go'n vote for the first black Congressman from Louisiana too, who will be no one other than our own Reverend Phillip J. Martin."

The people started to applaud, and Phillip raised his hands for silence. But the people would not be silent. Anthony McVay, the white attorney, standing on one side of Phillip, and Octave Bacheron, a white pharmacist, standing on the other side of him, each took one of his hands and held them high up in the air. And the applause was deafening.

After things had quieted down some, Howard Mills put on his overcoat and left the house. About a dozen other people left at the same time. But still the big living room remained noisy and crowded. Half the people were gathered round Phillip on one side of the room, the rest were in smaller groups throughout the house. Virginia's new tenant had moved. Now he was standing near the door that led out of the living room down the hall. But even when he moved he never took his eyes off Phillip Martin. Whenever someone got between them he would move again, never getting any closer, but always keeping Phillip in sight. Yet he did it so discreetly that no one, not even Shepherd, who stood next to him most of the time, was suspicious of anything. Beverly had joined them, and both Shepherd and she moved about the room with Virginia's tenant. They were never aware that he was doing this on purpose. They felt that it was the crowd pushing them into different places.

For the past few minutes Joyce Anne, Phillip's ten-year-old daughter, had been playing the piano. But there was so much noise in the room that no one paid any attention to her until Crystal McVay, the wife of the attorney, moved away from the crowd round Phillip and turned to the girl at the piano. Others in the room soon joined her. Elijah, who was Joyce Anne's teacher, stood behind the crowd with his tray of cups and glasses. Each time she played a difficult piece well he would shut his eyes and shake his head from side to side. But when she came to a part that might give her some trouble he would catch his breath and wait. Then when it was over, when she had done it in good form, he would sigh deeply (loud enough for others to hear), nod his head, and continue on through the crowd with his tray.

But not everyone near the piano was listening to the music. Phillip Martin was not. Neither to the music nor to the people round him. For the past couple of minutes he had been looking across the room where Shepherd, Beverly, and Virginia's tenant were standing. Shepherd, who had noticed it, didn't think Phillip was looking at them in particular. They were at opposite ends of the room, there were at least three dozen people between them, so he could have been looking at anyone in that direction. Still, he looked nowhere else. And even when someone would speak to him or touch him on the arm, he would give that person his attention only a moment, then look back cross the room again. He looked puzzled, confused, a deep furrow came into his forehead, and he raised his hand up to his temple as if he were in pain. Shepherd continued to watch him watching them. Suddenly he became very jealous. He knew of the minister's past reputation with women, so maybe he was eyeing Beverly now. Shepherd was angry for a moment, then he thought better of it, and he grinned at Phillip to let him know that he knew what was going on in his mind. But if Phillip saw him grin, he showed no sign that he did. Yet he looked only in that direction. When someone got between him and them, he craned his neck to see them better. Shepherd told Beverly what was going on.

"He's a handsome man, isn't he?" she said.

"Yes," Shepherd said. "And if I ever catch you anywhere near him somebody's getting hurt."

"Really?" she teased him.

"Really," he told her.

Phillip was not aware that they were talking about him, he was not aware that they were even looking at him; yet he continued to stare at them, the expression on his face still showing confusion.

Joyce Anne was bringing her third song to an end now, and the people were applauding her performance. But Phillip Martin was not hearing a thing. He pushed his way out of the crowd and started across the room. He had taken only two or three steps when he suddenly staggered and fell heavily to the floor.

The pharmacist, Octave Bacheron, was the first to reach him and told everyone else to stay back. But the people did not get back, they pressed in closer. Sister Aaron, whom Phillip had called on during his short speech, cried out that he had been poisoned, and soon the word was all over the house that he had been drugged. The little wife of Octave Bacheron, who was hard of hearing, kept asking who had fallen. The other white woman, the attorney's wife, told her that it was Phillip.

"Phillip drunk?" Phoebe Bacheron asked. "Phillip drunk?" She was a very small woman, and she had to lean her head back to look up at the people round her. "Phillip drunk?" she asked. "Phillip drunk?"

No one answered her. They moved in to look at Phillip on the floor. Virginia's new tenant was there with all the others. His reddish eyes narrowed, his face trembled as he stared down at him. It seemed for a moment that he might say something, maybe even scream, but he jerked away from the crowd and went out. He was the only one who left, but there was so much confusion in the room that no one paid him any attention.

Alma, who had rushed to Phillip when he fell, now knelt beside him holding his head up off the floor in her lap. He had lost consciousness only a moment, as a fighter might who has been hit hard on the jaw, but now he began recognizing people round him again, and he tried quickly, desperately, to push himself up. Octave Bacheron, who knelt on the other side of him, put his small white hand on Phillip's chest and told him to lie still a moment.

"I'm all right," he said to Octave Bacheron. "I'm all right," he said to Alma. He looked up at all the people standing over him. "I'm all right, I'm all right," he said to them.

"No," Octave Bacheron said, pressing his small white hand on his chest. "Be quiet a moment. Listen to me. Can you hear me, Phillip? Be quiet. Lie still a moment."

"I'm all right," Phillip said. The people who stood over him canopylike could see tears in his eyes. "I'm all right. Please let me up. I have to get up. Don't let me deny him again."

No one knew what he was talking about. No one asked him what he was talking about.

"You don't feel well, Phillip," Octave Bacheron said. "Listen, you don't feel well."

"Alma?" Phillip said. "Alma, please," he begged her. "I'm on the floor. I'm on the floor."

Octave Bacheron nodded to Anthony to help him get Phillip to his feet. Jonathan, who was closer to Phillip, took his arm, but Anthony pushed him roughly aside.

"What you think you doing?" Jonathan asked him.

"Helping your pastor," Anthony said.

"Ain't y'all done enough helping for one day?" Jonathan said. "That's why he's on his back now."

"Watch it, boy," Anthony said. "Watch your tongue there, now."

"Boy?" Jonathan said. "Boy?" He turned to the others in the room. "Y'all hear that, don't you? It's boy now. It's boy all over again."

"Please, Jonathan," Alma said. "Please. Phillip's on his back. Please."

Jonathan and Anthony glared at each other a moment, then Anthony turned to Phillip. Phillip told them again that he was all right and he could stand on his own. But the two white men insisted on helping him to his feet, and they made him lean on them as they followed Alma down the hall to the bedroom. Elijah, Joyce Anne, and another woman followed after them.

Everyone had deserted the two white women now. The smaller one, Phoebe, was crying and asking why was Phillip drunk. Why did he drink? Didn't he know drinking was no good? The other white woman did not try to explain but took Phoebe in her arms and patted her shoulders. The rest of the people watched the door and waited for some kind of news from the bedroom.

After about ten minutes, Octave Bacheron came back into the front. He told the people he believed that Phillip had fallen from exhaustion, but he was calling the doctor to be sure. He told them that both he and Alma would appreciate it if they did not take the rumor out of here that Phillip had been poisoned. Now, he wished that they would all get their coats and leave quietly, because their pastor needed rest more than anything else.

The doctor, a small clean-shaven bald man wearing a trench coat over a brown tweed suit, came to the house a half hour later. He was in the bedroom only a couple of minutes, then he wrote out a prescription for two bottles of pills. Elijah followed the pharmacist uptown and brought back the medicine.

Now that everyone else had gone, the house was deadly quiet. The doctor, repeating exactly what the pharmacist had said earlier, told Alma that what Phillip needed most was rest—quiet and rest. Alma, Elijah, and Joyce Anne sat in the living room talking so softly among themselves that they could hardly hear each other.

But things were quiet and peaceful only a short while, then the telephone started ringing. Elijah, who sat nearest the telephone, would try to reach it before it rang a second time. Everyone wanted to know what the doctor had said about Phillip. "He's tired and needs rest," Elijah told them. "Other than that he's fine. Fine. Fine. He just needs his rest." Elijah would hang up the telephone, but no sooner had he sat down it would ring again. Several people had heard that Phillip had been poisoned. "It's nothing like that," Elijah assured them. "Nothing like that. That's the kind of rumor we don't want out." Virginia Colar called from the boardinghouse. "You sure he's just tired?" she asked. "You sure he wasn't poisoned? You know how these white folks are. Remember President Kennedy, don't you? They ain't straightened that mess out yet—putting it all on poor Oswell. Remember King, don't you? Remember Long, don't you?" "I remember all of them," Elijah told her. "But Reverend Martin is just tired. Everybody ate the same food. Everybody drank out the same pot of eggnog, which I made myself. Mr. Octave drank out the same cup Reverend Martin drank from. Nothing happened to him." "And how you know it was the same cup?" Virginia asked. "You got to watch white folks. They sharp, them. Can switch a cup right 'fore your eyes and you'll never see it." "It was the same cup," Elijah said. "Reverend Martin's little blue-and-white china cup from Maison Blanche. I know that little cup like I know my name. He drinks out the same cup every day." "That's the trouble right there," Virginia said. "He drinks out the same little blue-and-white cup, and everybody know it. Can't they go to Maison Blanche and buy another little blue-and-white cup just like his?" "Listen, Virginia, now listen," Elijah said. "It was his little blue-and-white cup. His. Now, good night. I'll see you in church tomorrow."

Elijah sat up answering the telephone long after Alma and Joyce Anne had gone to bed. Then around midnight he went down the hall to his own room. He had been lying in bed wide awake for about an hour when he heard Alma and Phillip arguing out in the hall. Phillip had gotten out of bed and gone into his office, and Alma was trying to get him out of there. Elijah could hear her saying that she was going into the kitchen to warm up a glass of milk, because those pills weren't doing any good. He heard her passing by his room on her way into the kitchen, and a few minutes later he heard her going back up the hall again. It was quiet another hour, then more footsteps. Elijah listened for Alma's voice but didn't hear it. Now he called her, calling quietly: "Alma? Alma?" When she didn't answer, he got up and went to Phillip's office and knocked. It was quiet in the office, and Elijah pushed the door open and went in. Phillip sat behind his desk in the dark, facing the curtains over the window.

"Something the matter?" Elijah asked him.

"Thinking about service tomorrow," Phillip said without looking round.

"You ought to be in bed," Elijah said. "Let Jonathan conduct service tomorrow."

"I'm all right," Phillip said, still facing the curtains.

"The doctor want you to stay in bed," Elijah said.

Phillip didn't answer him.

"Reverend Martin, sir?"

"Leave me alone, will you," Phillip said, looking back over his shoulder. "I just want to sit here and think a while."

Elijah went back to his room and lay on top of the covers, but a few minutes later he was knocking on the office door again.

"Reverend Martin? Reverend Martin, sir?"

"All right," Phillip said, coming out. "Good night, Elijah."

5

Phillip Martin went back to bed, but he couldn't sleep. He lay wide awake for hours, listening to his wife snoring quietly beside him. He was trying not to think about the boy. He didn't want to think about him in here because he couldn't think clearly enough in here. The only place where he could think at all was in his office, but they came and got him out each time he went in there. He lay wide awake, hoping for tomorrow to hurry up and get here. Alma, Elijah, and Joyce Anne would go to church, and he would have the entire house to himself.

He didn't go to sleep until after daylight and he slept only about an hour. When he felt Alma waking up beside him he shut his eyes again and pretended to be still asleep. He heard her calling his name as she propped herself up on her elbow and leaned over him. When he didn't answer her, she got up, slipped into her robe, and quietly left the room. He lay in bed another half hour, then he got up, yawning loudly, and went into the kitchen where she was. Alma and Elijah sat at the table drinking coffee.

"I hope you don't think you going to any church today?" she said.

"I wasn't planning on it."

"I made sure of that already," Alma said. "Before Jonathan left from here last night I told him he was conducting service today."

"You told him?" Phillip asked her. "That's not your job. That's my job. That's Mills's job when I'm not there."

"When you start falling in front of a house of people, I make it my job," Alma said. "And I done already told Elijah when he go to church tell them people don't be coming here, and don't be calling on that phone neither. Doctor want you to rest, and you can't rest if that phone be ringing all the time."

"Ain't you going to church?" Phillip asked her.

"Joyce and Elijah going—I'm staying here," Alma said. "Leave, first thing I know you be in that office messing with papers."

"I got nothing in that office to do," Phillip said.

"You'd find something to do if I left from here."

Phillip looked to Elijah for help, but Elijah averted his eyes. Phillip turned back to Alma.

"No reason for you to stay here today," he said.

Alma didn't have any more to say about it, and Phillip left them and went back to bed. A few minutes later, Alma brought his breakfast and sat down on the bed to feed him. He told her he wasn't dying, neither was he an invalid, and he could feed himself. He didn't want the food at all, but he ate it just to keep her from worrying about him more. When he had finished eating she took away the tray and brought him the newspapers. He tried to read, but he could not keep his mind on the papers for thinking about the boy. But he didn't want to think about him in here. He had to get into his office. Only in there would he be able to sit and think and try to make some sense out of what had been going on the past week.

He folded the papers and laid them on the floor, then as he turned on his side to face the wall he heard Alma speaking to someone in the front room. A moment later she was opening the bedroom door to let Howard Mills come in. Mills wore a black overcoat with fur round the collar. He came into the room with his hat in his hand.

"Well, young fellow, how you feeling?" he asked Phillip.

Phillip nodded his head as he watched Mills come toward the bed. Mills pulled up a chair and sat down facing him.

"What happened?" Mills asked.

"I just went down," Phillip said, looking closely at Mills. He wondered what Mills would say if he really told him why he fell.

Mills looked suspiciously at Phillip. Phillip didn't look sick now, and surely he didn't look sick at all yesterday while he was at the party. He glanced over his shoulder toward the door, then looked back at Phillip again. Maybe Phillip would tell him if he was having some kind of problem. But Phillip had nothing to say.

Mills nodded his gray head. "Well, it happens to the best of us," he said.

"You think you and Jonathan can handle it all right?" Phillip asked him.

"Third Sunday—sure," Mills said. "He called me early this morning. We already went over what we have to do. I see Elijah's gone already?"

"Him and Joyce," Phillip said. "Alma's staying here with me."

Mills nodded his head. "How long the doctor keeping you in bed?" he asked.

"Couple days," Phillip told him.

"Couple days rest won't hurt you," Mills said.

The minister and the deacon looked closely at each other again. Phillip wanted to tell Mills, but he knew he could not. And Mills looking back at him knew that he had something on his mind.

"Well," he said, when he saw that Phillip wasn't going to say anything, "I better get on up there. See that Alcee get them heaters lit."

"Still cold out there?" Phillip asked him.

"Colder," Mills said, and stood up. He moved his chair back to the wall. "Something I wanted to say," he said. "Something. Something. Something about the party yesterday. But I can't remember now what it was. When you get this age you get a little minus every now and then."

"Had anything to do with Chenal?" Phillip asked him.

Mills shook his head. "No, I don't think so. Looked like it's something else."

"Well, it'll come to you," Phillip said.

"Yeah, in church," Mills said. "And by the time I leave church I be done forgot about it all over again. Ehh, when you get this old you get minus."

He grinned to himself. He twirled his hat on his finger. He looked at Phillip. Phillip didn't look weak at all. He wondered if Phillip had anything he wanted to say to him.

Phillip didn't say anything, and Mills nodded his head and went to the door.

"Have Jonathan remind the people about Chenal Friday," he said to Mills.

"I'm sure he'll bring it up," Mills said. "Think you'll be ready by then?"

"I'll be ready," Phillip said.

"Wouldn't want to face Chenal without you," Mills said.

"You won't," Phillip told him.

Mills nodded again and went out. Phillip could hear him and Alma talking in the hall. Alma was saying that she wished Mills would tell the people not to call or visit for a day or two. Mills said he understood and would bring it up in church.

Phillip lay on his side facing the wall. He wondered what it was that Mills wanted to talk about. He wondered if it was about the boy. But, no, how could it be? If Mills had known who the boy was he would have brought it up yesterday.

Again in his mind's eye he saw the boy's thin, bearded face watching him from across the room. At first he paid it little attention, but after noticing it each time he looked in that direction he began to ask himself why. Who was he? How did he get in here? Who invited him? He was sure he had never seen him anywhere before. He would look away a moment to answer someone's question, but when he looked back across the room he would find the boy still watching him as if no time whatever had passed. Why? he asked himself. Why? Who is he?

Then he remembered having heard about a stranger in St. Adrienne. The stranger had sat behind his church door the first night that he was here. Several people had seen him passing by the house. One or two had even seen him standing out in the street watching the house. Yes, and now that he remembered, Elijah had said something about inviting him to the party. But why was he standing there watching him? Why?

Then he knew. Even when he told himself no, it couldn't be so, he knew definitely that it was. The dream that he had a night or two before the boy got here was more than a dream, it was a vision, an omen, a warning.

Phillip pressed his face down against the sheet and tried not to think about it any more. Let him think about anything else but not about this. Think about Chenal. Chenal wasn't going to be easy. Chenal knew the people needed work. Even if he paid them less than minimum they still had to work for him, because there weren't any other jobs. Phillip wondered what he would do if Chenal said no to their demands. Demonstrate against the store? Yes. What else? But suppose Chenal fired the people working for him, then what? They could eventually close down Chenal if the people demonstrated long enough against the store, but where would they work during that time?

Phillip Martin felt tired and confused. He looked at the two little bottles of pills and the glass of water on the small lamp table by the bed. He picked up one of the bottles and started to unscrew the cap, then threw it back. He wanted to knock everything on the floor, but he knew Alma would hear the noise and come into the room.

Just before noon he went to sleep again. When he woke up a couple of hours later he heard the piano in the living room. Joyce Anne and Elijah had come back from church, and Joyce Anne was playing the piano while Alma and Elijah were talking. They kept their voices down to keep from disturbing him.

Phillip started thinking about the boy again. Why? he asked himself. Why after all these years—why? And how did he know where to find me? Did she send him here? And if she did, why this game? Why sit behind the church door? Why for a week walk the street and watch the house? Come into the house, watch me, but say nothing—why? What's he want? What's he up to? He's got to be up to something. What?

Phillip heard Alma and Joyce Anne talking in the hall, and he shut his eyes only a moment before Alma came into the room and asked him if he was still asleep. He didn't answer her, but he could tell that she was standing there watching him. Then he heard her crossing the room to the dresser where she sat before the mirror to brush her hair. He would hear a few strokes of the brush, then a moment of silence as if she might be watching him through the mirror; then he would hear the brush again. After she had gotten her overcoat out of the closet, she came to the bed and kissed him and left the room. He could hear her telling Elijah not to dare leave from here until she got back. He figured that she and Joyce Anne were going on the Island to her mother to get the other two children, Patrick and Emily.

Phillip stayed in bed until he heard the car backing out of the yard, then he got up and put on his robe. Elijah was at the piano now, playing quietly, and only with one hand. Phillip stood by the door listening a moment, then when he was sure Elijah had not heard him moving round in the room, he hurried across the hall into his office.

His office was a small, dark, cold room, with heavy brown curtains over the window. A desk, two chairs, and a file cabinet made up the furniture. On the wall facing the desk was a large picture of the crucifixion. On the left was a collage of President John Kennedy, Robert Kennedy, and Martin Luther King. In another frame hanging evenly with the first was another collage, of Abraham Lincoln, Frederick Douglass, and Booker T. Washington. Across the room on the right wall were Phillip's diploma from Bible school, a 1970 calendar from the local mortuary, and a picture of Phillip and his deacons standing before the church. The men were all dressed in dark suits, their hats in their hands, looking severely at the camera. Howard Mills, whose head was nearly snow white, stood a couple of inches taller than anyone else.

The room was dark and cold, but Phillip wouldn't turn on the light or light the heater. He went directly to the window and pulled back the curtains to look out on the street. Where was the boy? Where was he this moment? Why wasn't he passing the house? Phillip had heard that he walked the streets day and night, whether it was raining or not, whether it was cold or not—then where was he now?

Phillip stood at the window looking and waiting. But Virginia's new tenant did not go by the house. No one passed by walking or driving. There was nothing out there but a leafless pecan tree in the open pasture across the street.

Phillip would not move from the window. Now he was thinking about the dream he'd had the night before the boy got there. In the dream he was sitting on the side of the bed, just as he'd been doing twenty-one years ago. In the dream, just as it had happened that day, he saw the boy's small hand in the crack of the door as he took the money from the woman. He left with the money, but soon brought it back. When he left the second time, Phillip got up from the bed and ran after him. In the dream it happened like that, but twenty-one years ago he hadn't run after the boy at all. He had sat on the bed looking down at the floor until he was sure the boy had gone, then he went to the woman who was still clutching the money, tore it out of her hand, and threw it into the fire. When the woman tried to get the money out of the fire with her bare hands, he slapped her so hard that she fell halfway cross the room. She came back, not for the money, the money had burned, she came back fighting. This time he hit her with his fist. Then he went to the bed and sat down, burying his face in his hands and crying. But in the dream they did not fight. In the dream he told her the money was hers, she could do whatever she wanted with it, and he ran out of the house to catch the boy. The boy had already gotten on the wagon along with his mother and other brother and sister, and Chippo Simon was driving them to the road to catch the bus. Phillip could see Johanna calling to him; he could see the oldest boy reaching out his small arms. But the other two children sitting in the bed of the wagon neither saw anything nor heard anything.

Phillip woke from the dream screaming, his bedclothes wet with perspiration. He didn't go back to sleep at all that night, and the next day while sitting behind his desk in the office he quit his reading or writing several times to reflect on the dream again. He could still see Johanna in the black overcoat and black hat waving her arms and calling to him. But why black? Why black? He had never known her to wear anything but the brightest colors when she was here. Why black now? He could still see the oldest boy at the tailgate of the wagon reaching out his small arms. But the other two children went on playing as if nothing was happening round them. He ran as hard as he could to catch them, but the wagon slowly and steadily moved farther and farther away.

Phillip stood at the window looking out on the street, looking and waiting. But the boy didn't go by. No one went by. The street, gray, empty, cold. The tree in the pasture across the street, gray, leafless, cold.

Phillip turned from the window to his desk. He wanted to pray, he needed to pray, but how could he pray? If he prayed out loud, Elijah would surely hear him; and he could not get satisfaction praying in silence.

The Bible on his desk was opened to the fourteenth chapter of John. He had chosen today's sermon from that chapter. He began reading, moving his lips as he read: "Let not your heart be troubled; ye believe in God, believe also in me. In my Father's house are many mansions; if it were not so, I would have told you. I go to prepare a place for you. And if I go—" He stopped. He turned back to the window and pulled the curtains to the side.

Who could he go to? Who would believe him? Mills? Would Mills believe him if he told Mills he had fallen because he recognized his boy across the room? Or would he feel the same way the others did, that he had fallen because he was tired?

Tired? Tired? He, Phillip Martin, tired? He could have picked up both Octave Bacheron and Anthony McVay at the same time. He could have pushed that piano across the room with both of them sitting on top of it. Tired? Tired? He, Phillip Martin, tired?

Why did he do it? Why did he lie there and let them say that? Did they ask him if he was tired? Did they ask his wife anything? Why did he let them do this to himself, do this to his people? Why didn't he knock that white man's hand away from his chest? He could have done it easily as flicking away a fly. Wouldn't that have been the right thing for him to do—brushing away that white man's hand and getting to his feet? Being leader, wasn't that the thing to do? If not the leader, who then? Who?

But no, like some cowardly frightened little nigger, he lay there and let them do all the talking for him. He even let them push pills down in his mouth. Here's a white pill, here's a pink pill, take that and stay quiet. Rest, rest, rest a few days and you'll be back doing your work again. What work? What work? Getting up off the floor, without their help, that was the work he should have done.

His back was to the window now, and he was looking at the pictures on the wall. These great men always gave him encouragement when he was troubled. In his heart he asked them now for guidance. He prayed quietly to the picture of Christ on the cross.

He turned back to the window and looked out on the street again. But no one was passing by his house.

He could hear Elijah at the piano. Should he go to Elijah? But say what to Elijah? Say what to Elijah today that he couldn't say yesterday, or last night when Elijah called him out of the office? Say what to Elijah that he couldn't even say to his own wife? Or to Mills whom he had known all of his life? No, no. He must first talk to the boy. He had to find out why he was there. Did his mother send him? He was too young when he left from there to remember, so she must have sent him. But sent him for what? For what? And why the game?

Phillip went out of the office and stood in the door between the hall and the living room. Elijah had just finished one song, and he was turning a page in the hymnal to begin another when Phillip spoke to him.

"Always practicing, Elijah?"

Elijah jerked around, his hand slamming down on the piano keys. He nearly fell off the stool when he saw Phillip standing only a few feet away from him.

"Didn't mean to scare you," Phillip said. "I had been

listening to your music from the bedroom. Just thought I'd come in here to listen better."

"Alma want you to stay in bed, sir," Elijah said, after he had caught his breath. "She went on the island to get the children. Told me to make sure you stayed in bed."

"I'm all right," Phillip said.

He went to the front door and pulled the curtains to the side. He looked through the glass and through the screened porch. But no one stood in the street watching his house, and no one was passing by.

"Something the matter?" Elijah asked him.

"I'm checking the weather," Phillip said.

"Sure to freeze tonight," Elijah told him.

"How was church?" Phillip asked, turning from the door and facing Elijah again.

"Church was all right."

"Alcee lit the heaters on time?"

"It was still a little chilly when I got there," Elijah said. "Most of the people kept their coats on."

"How did Jonathan make out?" Phillip asked.

"All right," Elijah said. "But Jonathan is still a little too"—Elijah touched the side of his head—"too sophisticated for the people—especially the old people. They feel Jonathan is talking over them, not to them."

"Jonathan is that new breed," Phillip said. "He thinks education, big words, is all you need to communicate. He'll have to learn he must break them big words down to reach his people. They all right in school, but not in that church, and not out there on the street either. What did he talk about?"

"The work mostly. Chenal Friday."

"Did the people ask about me?"

"Everybody," Elijah said.

"What did you tell them?"

"You fell because you were tired."

"Do I look tired to you, Elijah?" Phillip asked him.

"Sir?"

Phillip stood wide-legged and stretched out his two big arms. In his navy blue cotton robe, he looked like a heavyweight fighter in the center of the ring.

"Do I look tired?" he asked again.

"That's what the doctor said," Elijah said.

"Yes, that's what the doctor said," Phillip said. "But Octave Bacheron said it first."

"Mr. Bacheron studied medicine," Elijah said. "I think—"

"Octave Bacheron studied pills," Phillip cut him off. "Pills, not medicine. White pills and pink pills. There's a difference, Elijah."

Elijah thought Phillip was speaking strangely, and he felt embarrassed and lowered his eyes.

"First time I ever fell in my life," Phillip told him. "No, the second time. The first time was that Thursday morning when He lifted the burden of sin from my shoulders. I swooned, I fell." Phillip thought back to that moment of his conversion fifteen years ago and nodded, thoughtfully, to himself. "The only other time I ever fell in my life," he said. "Shot at; shot. Staggered, but wouldn't go down. I was a good man, boy; I was a good man." He frowned and squeezed his forehead.

"Something the matter?" Elijah asked again.

"Just thinking about being a man," Phillip said. "Just thinking about being a man. Men supposed to clamb up off the floor."

"Not if you're tired, sir," Elijah said.

"Floyd Patterson was tired," Phillip said. "Did you see that fight? How many times that Swede knocked him down? Six, seven times? But he got up. He kept on getting up. I fell once—and I let a little finger—I coulda knocked that hand away like, like knocking lint off my robe." He flicked at imaginary lint on the sleeve of his robe. "Why didn't I, Elijah? And don't say I was tired."

"Yes sir," Elijah said.

"Then why didn't I?"

"I don't know, sir."

"Because he's white? And that's why y'all believed without questioning—because he's white?"

"At that time, what else could we believe, sir?" Elijah asked.

"Nothing else," Phillip said. "I don't know why I'm blaming y'all. I'm the one to blame."

"For what, sir? For falling?"

"For denying him twice," Phillip said.

"Denying who, sir?"

Phillip shook his head. He couldn't say any more now than he could say last night.

"It was a nice party," he said.

"I thought so," Elijah agreed.

"You had a lot of people. Didn't expect to see so many in this kind of weather."

"They came for a good cause, Reverend Martin."

"You still think so, Elijah?"

"I know so," Elijah said.

"Lately I've been having my doubts," Phillip said. "Since Martin's death—I don't know. The older people still there—but where's the young? If you not reaching the young, what good you doing?"

"You've done a lot of good, Reverend Martin," Elijah said.

"Have done, Elijah?"

"Still doing, sir."

"Leaders have to clamb up off the floor," Phillip said. "We can't let others speak for us no more, Elijah."

"You speak for us, Reverend Martin," Elijah said trying to encourage him.

"I didn't speak for you yesterday," Phillip said. "I reckon it's no sin to fall. But surely it's one not to get up."

He turned from Elijah and looked out on the street

again. Where was the boy? In his room? Walking the streets? Where?

"Did your friend show up?" Phillip asked, with his back to Elijah. "That new tenant at Virginia's house?"

"He was here," Elijah said. "Him, Shep, Beverly stood cross the room over there most of the time."

Phillip turned back to Elijah, pretending he didn't know what he was talking about.

"Stood where?" he asked.

Elijah nodded his head toward the other side of the room. "Over there," he said.

"Wait," Phillip said. "Wait. I think I did see him. He wore an overcoat, and a wool cap?"

"That was Robert X," Elijah said.

"Robert X?" Phillip asked.

Elijah nodded. "That's what he calls himself—Robert X. But if he's a Muslim, he sure doesn't carry himself like one."

"Why would he call himself Robert X then?" Phillip asked. "Hiding from something?"

"I don't know," Elijah said. "According to him he's on his way to a conference—some kind of black man's conference. He stopped off here to meet somebody."

"To meet who?"

Elijah shrugged his shoulders. "I have no idea."

"Y'all talked, and he never mentioned a name, not once?"

"No sir, not once," Elijah said.

"Maybe Shepherd knows?"

"I don't think so," Elijah said. "Shep woulda told me if he knew. It's none of my business, but I don't think he's here to meet anybody. I think he's just drifting. Just drifting. I think he's a lost soul that's just drifting."

"How do you mean?" Phillip asked.

"Plain lost," Elijah said. "Psychologically lost. Lonely. Nowhere to go. The other day when I gave him a ride he said nothing matters to him. He said winter and summer were the same. Good weather or bad weather it didn't matter. It's none of my business, but it looks like he wouldn't care if he died tomorrow. I don't think he'd care if he caught pneumonia and died tomorrow. When you look in his face you see somebody who don't care any more."

Listening to Elijah, a heaviness came in Phillip's chest. His heart started beating a little too fast. He felt his eyes burning him and he wanted to raise his hand, but he knew Elijah was still watching him.

"I want to meet him," he said. "Can you get him to come back—I mean with Shepherd and the others?"

"If I see him I'll tell him," Elijah said. "But he didn't act like he wanted to come the first time. He didn't think he was good enough for a house like this. I told him this house was opened to everybody."

"Yes," Phillip said. "Any time. Any time he would like to come here. Any time. Tell him I said so myself."

"I'll take a little run up to the Congo Room when Alma gets back," Elijah said. "If I see him I'll tell him then."

Phillip went back into his office. Behind him he heard Elijah saying that he ought to be in bed, but he didn't answer. He went into the room and stood by the window looking out on the street.

What is his name? he asked himself. What is his name? Robert is not his name, I'm sure of that. What is his name? What is his name?

He spent the rest of the afternoon in his office, either standing at the window, sitting at his desk, or pacing the floor. No matter what name he came up with he could not be sure that it was his son's name. He tried remembering the names of the other two children, but he couldn't remember theirs either. He thought about all the names of the old people, both in his and Johanna's families. But still he couldn't be sure who the children were named for. He looked in the Bible, but he could not read, and he turned to the window again.

Just before dark he saw the small station wagon turn into the yard, and he hurried out of the office into the bedroom. He had just hung up his robe and gotten under the covers when he heard Alma and the children come inside the house. Alma pushed the bedroom door open and asked him if he was asleep, and when he told her no, she called in the children to speak to him. Patrick, wearing a black overcoat and mittens, came up to the bed quickly, bravely, and shook hands. Emily in her red overcoat and red bonnet seemed afraid and stood back, until Phillip smiled at her, then she came up to the bed and kissed him on the mouth. Joyce Anne kissed her father on the forehead, then she led her smaller brother and sister out of the room.

"You all right, Phillip?" Alma asked him. She sat down on the bed and passed her hand over the side of his face. His day-old beard felt and sounded like sandpaper to her.

"I'm all right," he said.

"You sure you all right, Phillip?"

"I'm all right. How'd you leave everybody?"

"Everybody's fine. Daddy wanted to come over and see you, but I told him to wait a couple days."

She got up from the bed to hang up her coat in the closet.

"You having supper with us?" she asked.

"Yes. I'm tired of this bed."

"You stayed in bed all day?"

"Got up once; went to the bathroom. What time did you go on the Island?"

"After Joyce and Elijah came back from church."

"I musta been asleep," he said.

"I'll call you when it's time to eat," Alma said, and left the room.

A half hour later Emily knocked on the door and told

him that supper was on the table. When he came into the kitchen everyone, including Elijah, was sitting round the table waiting for him. He sat down and blessed the food.

Both Emily and Patrick watched him constantly. Alma had already explained to them that he had fallen from overwork, but they couldn't understand it. They had never heard of a man falling from overwork, and they had never known him to be sick before.

While the children watched him, Phillip looked at Elijah to see if Elijah had said anything to Alma about his being up all afternoon. But Elijah seemed innocent enough, and Alma didn't seem suspicious of anything either.

After supper Phillip took the pills in front of everyone to let them see that he was following the doctor's orders. Then he left the table and went into the bedroom to get the newspapers. When Elijah came into the living room with his hat and overcoat, Phillip was sitting in a dark-brown soft-leather chair pretending to be reading. He was not reading, he had been sitting there the last few minutes thinking about his son. He knew that Robert was not his name. And he had been sitting there trying to think of his true name.

"You going out?" he asked Elijah.

"The Congo Room for a quick one," Elijah said.

"If you see Shepherd, Beverly, tell them I'm sorry I didn't get to see them yesterday. They might want to drop by again soon."

"I'll tell them," Elijah said.

Phillip didn't mention Virginia's new tenant. He hoped that Elijah would remember their conversation earlier that afternoon.

After Elijah had gone, Phillip went to the door to look outside again. It was dark now, and he wouldn't have been able to tell his boy from anyone else even if he had passed by the house. When he heard Alma coming up the hall, he sat down in his chair and pretended to be reading.

Alma came into the room with her sewing basket and

a pair of khaki pants. Phillip watched her sit by a light near the fireplace.

"Something for Patrick?" he asked her.

"A brand-new pair pants he tore playing cowboy," Alma said. "I told them they can watch television after they finish their lesson."

Phillip looked across the room at her a while, then he started thinking about the boy again. He was trying to figure out how he had found out where he was. Had someone from St. Adrienne or from Reno Plantation gone up North recently? Had Johanna written home and asked about him? How else would the boy have known where to find him?

Why? he asked himself. He had asked himself this a dozen times at least. After all these years—why? The boy was what now—twenty-seven? twenty-eight? Twenty-seven, because he was born the winter of '42. Cane cutting—grinding. Because she had cut cane all day Saturday, and the boy was born on Sunday. He didn't see him for a week, because he wasn't living with her. He lived with his parents in one house, and she lived with her mother and sister farther down the quarters. He saw the baby a week later when she brought him to the gate wrapped in a blanket. A year later there was another boy, and a year after that a little girl. They still lived separately. He had no time for marriage, for settling down. There were too many other things to do; there were too many other women in his life.

"Something in that paper must be good," he heard Alma saying. "You ain't turned that page once."

"Nixon," he said, without looking at her.

"What's he up to now?"

"Same thing. Still messing over people."

Alma went on with her sewing. Phillip watched her a moment, then flipped the page of the newspaper. He tried reading a couple of minutes, but soon his mind began wandering again.

He remembered the day Johanna and the children left

from there. It was cold, raining, just as it was now. It was either December, 1948, or January, 1949, because he was living with Tut Hebert at the time. He remembered that he had been gambling the night before they left, and he had lost everything but three dollars, which he had stuffed down into his watch pocket, something to give each child just in case he saw them again before they left.

That was over twenty years ago. He hadn't sent her one penny or written her one letter in all that time, and neither had he received a letter from her. He had heard that she lived in Texas a few years, then she left for California. He had not heard a thing about her since.

Why now? he asked himself again. Why now?

When Elijah came back to the house around nine thirty, the children had studied their lesson, had watched a show on television, and had gone to bed. Alma had put up her sewing and she was back in the kitchen making coffee. Phillip sat in the living room alone, with half of the newspaper in his lap and the rest on the floor by his chair.

"Getting colder and colder out there," Elijah said. "Freeze before morning."

He took off his hat and coat and laid them on the arm of the couch. Then he went to the fireplace and stood with his back to the fire. Phillip looked at him, waiting to hear if he had seen the boy.

"Alma turned in?" Elijah asked.

"In the kitchen," Phillip said.

Elijah blew on his hands and rubbed them. Phillip looked at him, waiting. Elijah turned his back on Phillip and held his hands over the fire.

"You caught up with your friends?" Phillip asked when it seemed that Elijah wasn't going to say anything.

"Up there drinking as usual," Elijah said, still holding his hands over the fire.

"You told them what I said?"

"Tuesday evening, after school," Elijah said, and turned round to face Phillip again.

"Who-all you saw?" Phillip asked casually.

"The usual crowd—Shep, Beverly, Guy, Frances, Chuck. Yes—Robert X was sitting there with them, drinking wine. Everybody else drinking Old Forester, Robert X drinking wine."

"Wine?" Phillip said.

"Yes sir. Wine."

"Well, if he come maybe we'll have a little wine Tuesday," Phillip said. "Yes, a little wine. They said they was coming?"

"They'll probably show up," Elijah said. "They don't do nothing else in the evening but sit around and drink."

Alma came into the living room with three cups of coffee, a bowl of sugar, a small pitcher of cream, and a plate of cookies on a tray. She served Phillip, then Elijah, and set the tray on the coffee table in front of the couch. Elijah came to the couch with his cup of coffee and sat down.

"What was all that talking about up here?" Alma asked Phillip. "I thought you was supposed to be resting."

"We was just talking about the teachers," Phillip said. "I told Elijah to invite them to the house. They coming over Tuesday evening."

"Who say you can have company that soon?" Alma asked him. "I told my own people you needed rest, now you inviting others?"

"The doctor said rest a couple days," Phillip told her. "Today is one; tomorrow two; all day Tuesday is three. If I needed any more rest than that they might as well put me in the grave."

"That's where you'll be if you don't start listening to people," Alma said. She turned on Elijah, who was sitting at the other end of the couch. "You the one doing this behind my back?" she asked him.

"Don't blame Elijah," Phillip said from across the room. He drank from the hot coffee and set the cup back in the saucer that he held in the palm of his hand. "I didn't get a chance to talk with Shepherd and Beverly yesterday, and I told Elijah to invite them back."

"Can't it wait till you up and moving around?"

"I'll be up and moving around Tuesday," he said.

"And what the doctor say don't mean a thing?"

"I'm tired hearing about that doctor," Phillip said. "Right now I'm stronger than that little Cajun ever was or ever will be."

"That little Cajun didn't fall in front of a house full of people yesterday," Alma said.

"How do you know?" Phillip asked her. "He mighta fell a dozen times 'fore he got here. He didn't look too strong to me."

Alma stared at Phillip across the room. The longer she looked at him, the angrier she got. She started to speak, but she changed her mind and left the room. Phillip and Elijah heard her slam the bedroom door down the hall.

"She'll get over it," Phillip said. "Listen, I want you to get me two bottles of wine."

"Wine?" Elijah said, looking at Phillip as if he couldn't believe what Phillip was telling him to do. "Alma's already mad at me, Reverend Martin."

"I can handle Alma," Phillip said. "Two bottles of good wine. Sherry. Your friend is right. The rest of them ought to get off that hard stuff. No good for your liver. Turn it green. What they sell that stuff now? That good stuff?"

"I don't know," Elijah said. "Five, six dollars, I reckon."

"I want the best," Phillip said. He was elated with the thought that he would see the boy on Tuesday. "Go up to Lorio's," he said. "I'm sure he has some good stuff up there. Tell him you want the best. Tell him it's for me. Tell him I want the same kind he sell them priests when they having a party."

Elijah lowered his head. Phillip sounded to him as if he had had a few drinks already.

Phillip raised the coffee cup to his mouth, while thinking about the boy. In his mind's eye he already saw him sitting there on the couch. He would let him sit there a while with his glass of wine, then he would get him to follow him to another part of the house. There, alone, they would talk. They might even go in the yard and walk across the lawn, or they might even go for a ride in the car.

But talk about what? Talk about what? Phillip asked himself. They were total strangers. The boy was his son by blood only. How many times had he held him in his arms? How many times had he ridden him on his back? He couldn't recall now if he ever did. He couldn't even recall his true name.

Talk about what then?

He would ask about Johanna. Yes. Yes. He would ask about Johanna. He would ask about her.

She was a beauty, that woman, when she was young. That good, light-brown café-au-lait color. She never had to put makeup on that face; no iron in that hair. No, not with that skin and that hair. Hair like silk. Yes. Natural. Natural as any flower, any rose. She was a natural. That's what she was, a natural, a natural beauty. So different from all the others, so much better than all the others. Yes, he could still remember her. After all these years, he could still remember her.

"Sir?" he heard Elijah saying.

Phillip looked at him. He didn't know he was still there.

"What?" he asked.

"You want me to take these things in the back?" Elijah said, as if he had asked the same question some time ago.

Phillip nodded his head. "Sure, you can take them back. Good night, Elijah."

After Elijah had gone with the tray, he sat there another ten or fifteen minutes drinking his coffee, which was cold now. Finally, he got up, turned out the lights, and went down the hall to the bedroom. Alma sat on the side of the bed looking down at the floor. He sat down on the bed beside her, but he didn't say anything for a while.

Then he asked, "You mad 'cause I invited Elijah's friends to the house?"

"You coulda asked me," she said.

"I was go'n tell you when you came in the front. You didn't give me time."

Alma turned on him. She was still angry. "Not tell me," she said. "Not tell me, Phillip. Ask me. This is my house too. Ask me sometime, Phillip."

"You want me to go in there and tell Elijah not to bring his friends to the house? I'll go in there right now if that's what you want."

He knew she would say no, even when he was saying it. She shook her head and looked down at the floor again.

"Why don't you get in bed," he told her. "I'll look after the children."

He went to both rooms. Patrick slept alone. The girls had single beds in another room. Everyone was asleep. Phillip tucked the covers well, kissed each child, and left. He went back to the front door and pulled the curtains to the side, but it was too dark now to see anything out there. When he came back into the bedroom he found Alma still sitting on the bed.

"If you go'n sit up, I might as well stay up with you," he told her.

She undressed, then got into bed, facing the wall. He lay down beside her and tried to talk to her, but she wouldn't answer. After a while she fell off to sleep. But for hours he lay there as wide awake as he had been all day.

Between one and two o'clock he got up again, went into his office, and pulled back the curtains. The lawn was white with frost. The pecan tree in the open pasture across the street stood bare and alone. But no one stood out in front of the house, and no one was passing by. He turned from the window and knelt down beside his desk to pray. But when he got up off his knees he felt as if he had not prayed at all. He looked out of the window again, then he went back to bed, but knowing very well that he would not sleep.

When Alma took the children to school the next morning, he went back into his office again. Elijah had gone, and he had the entire house to himself. Before kneeling, he opened the Bible to the book of Psalms and read one verse from the one hundred second chapter. "Hear my prayer, O Lord, and let my cry come unto thee. Hide not thy face from me in the day when I am in trouble; incline thine ear unto me." He stopped here, reread the words silently to himself, thought about them a moment, then knelt beside the desk facing the picture of the crucifixion. But he didn't begin with the Lord's Prayer as he usually did each day, and neither did he say any of the things that he had said daily since his conversion. Instead, he asked the same question over and over: "Why? Why? Why? Is this punishment for my past? Is that why he's here, to remind me? But I asked forgiveness for my past. And You've forgiven me for my past."

He sat back on his legs, facing the crucifixion.

"Why, Father?" Phillip Martin asked. "Why? I think I've served You well; I think I've served my people well. Why?" he asked. "Why?"

The thorn-crowned, twisted, bleeding body of Christ hung on the cross, mute.

"Turn not thine ear from me in the day that I am troubled," Phillip Martin prayed.

He was in the kitchen when Alma came back to the house. He had just set a kettle of water over one of the front burners, and he was still at the stove when Alma came in with the newspapers.

"How long you been up?" she asked him.

"I'm just getting up," he said.

She gave him the papers, then she went to the stove to cook his breakfast. He sat at the table reading quietly to himself. He had gone through half of the papers when he came upon a very short story that he read out loud to her. Two white boys hunting rabbits had found the corpse of a black boy in a ditch of water between New Orleans and Laplace. The boy had been dead several days and his body frozen. The police didn't find any identification on the body, and nobody knew who he was.

Alma shook her head, sadly, but didn't say anything. Phillip read the story again. When Alma brought his breakfast to the table he was staring at the paper but not reading.

"He's just another X," he said, looking up at Alma. "He's just another X, that's all."

He ate his breakfast without wanting it. He took a pill from each bottle, hating the pills, and hating himself for taking them. After a while he went into the living room and looked out on the street. He wanted to go into his office, but he knew Alma would come in there and get him out.

He sat down in the big leather chair with his pipe. The pipe was a birthday present from his children a year ago. He had smoked it a few times the first week and hadn't picked it up again for a month. Even now he sucked on the pipe without lighting it.

Alma had been singing in the kitchen while she worked, but suddenly the singing stopped, and Phillip knew why. She thought he had gone into his office, and now she was listening. A moment later he heard her coming up to the front.

"No, I'm not in there," he told her. "But I need to get out of here, if just out there in the yard."

"I don't want you catching cold out there," she said.

"I won't catch cold. I'll wear my overcoat," he told her.

He went into the bedroom and dressed. He still had the pipe when he came back into the kitchen. He used the end of a matchstick to light the pipe from a burner on the stove.

"Don't be out there too long," she said.

"I won't."

Before going out the door he reached over and patted her twice on the butt.

"Doctor said a week," she said.

"What?"

"A week."

"I didn't hear him say that."

"He whispered in my ear. Said none for a week. I might give you a relapse."

"That doctor must think you pretty wild," Phillip said.

"I do all right," Alma said.

Phillip grinned at her. "You do better than all right, Little Mama," he told her. "But we cutting that time in half. I hope you ready. You go'n have a lot of work to do."

"I'll be ready."

"I will too," he said.

He started out of the door again.

"Phillip?" she said.

He looked back at her.

"I want you to come to me sometime, Phillip," she said. She had been playing before, but she was serious now.

"Don't I come to you?" he said.

"Not just for that, Phillip."

"I don't want you mixed up out there," he said.

"That's my job, too, Phillip."

"I want you in here," he said.

"I'm in here all the time," she said. "But you don't come to me. You go in that room. You go out there in the yard. I'm in here—but you never come to me."

He didn't know how to answer her. He didn't even try. He nodded his head and went out.

The back yard was surrounded by a tall cypress fence. Small maple and elm trees had been planted inside the fence all the way round the yard. The top of the trees, two or three feet above the pickets, waved softly from a slight wind off the St. Charles River. Phillip fastened the top button of his coat, not because he was cold, but because Alma might look outside and tell him to do so. Walking across the yard, with one hand in his coat pocket and the other holding the pipe in his mouth, he could feel the thick, springy St. Augustine grass under his shoes. When he came up to the back fence he turned and looked at the house again. He was proud of this house. He had worked hard for his family, his church, the people and the movement, and he had been proud of that hard work. He thought he had done a good job, at least both black and white had told him so. But now, after seeing the boy in the house, after falling and not getting up, he had begun to question himself; Who really was Phillip Martin, and what, if anything, had he really done?

He stood there looking at the house and thinking about the boy. The cold wind off the river burning his face didn't matter. He probably would have stood there an hour if he had not seen Alma pull back the curtain and look out of the window at him. He started walking again. The pipe had gone out, but that didn't matter either.

Out of all the things I've come up against these past few years—this one, this one, this one, Phillip Martin thought as he walked across the yard. Where do I start? he asked himself. What do I do? Go up to Virginia? Say what when I get up there? I demand to know why you here? Demand? Demand? After twenty years—more than twenty years—what give me the right to demand? Ignore him like I did in the past? Pretend he's not even there? If that was possible, I never woulda fell. No, no, something is happening in me. Something is challenging me. Why? Why?

When Phillip came to the other end of the yard at the side of the house, he looked out toward the street. But a tall cypress gate between the house and the fence blocked the street from him. He stared at the gate now as if someone or something had put it there that very moment to keep him from seeing the boy.

Alma, who had been watching him through the window all the time, saw him standing there looking toward the street. When he didn't move after a few minutes, she left the window and went to the door to call him. He didn't answer her. She called him again. But instead of answering he started walking toward the front of the house. When she caught up with him he was standing at the gate gripping it with both hands.

"Didn't you hear me calling you?" she asked. "Phillip? Phillip?"

"I heard you," he said.

"Why didn't you answer me?"

"I was thinking. I can think, can't I?"

"Come on inside," she said. "It's getting cold out here."

He shook the gate hard with both hands. But the gate of cypress was too solidly built to rattle.

"Phillip?" Alma said. "Phillip?"

He slammed his weight against it, then turned quickly away.

"First thing I do when I start moving round is take that thing down," he said.

"Take it down for what?" she asked him.

" 'Cause I put it there," he said.

6

Tuesday after school, Shepherd and Elijah went uptown to get two bottles of wine. On their way back, they went by Virginia's boardinghouse. When Elijah asked her if her new tenant was in his room, she said she didn't know because she hadn't seen him in two days, but she did know one thing, he had a gun up there, a .38 revolver, wrapped in a brown paper bag.

They stood just inside the door. Both Shepherd and Elijah wore overcoats and hats. Virginia wore a sweater over her dress and a bandanna on her head. The ends of the bandanna were tied into a tight little knot over her forehead.

"That person he come here to meet he come here to kill," she said, speaking low and nodding her head for emphasis. She looked at Shepherd, then Elijah, nodding to both of them. "That," she said, "or there ain't nobody else, and he come here to kill himself."

"I don't believe that," Shepherd said.

But he could remember their talking in the room last Saturday, and if he was serious about half of the things he said, then Shepherd believed he could do almost anything.

"Then what's he doing here?" Virginia asked Shepherd. "Tell me that."

"Maybe he just come here to see somebody like he said."

He didn't believe this either. And Virginia looking in his face could see he didn't believe it.

"Me and you both know better than that," she said.

"I don't know no more than what he said," Shepherd said. "He said he come here to meet somebody, that's what I believe."

Virginia nodded her head. She knew he was lying. She could tell by his face, his eyes, he was lying. He tried not looking directly at her, but she watched him all the time.

"I told him when he first got here I didn't want no trouble in my place," she said. "I sure don't want no killing up there—himself or nobody else."

"Nobody's going to get killed, Virginia," Shepherd said.

"How do you know?"

He wouldn't look at her. He didn't know how to answer her. He could still remember the conversation in the room last Saturday. He was still asking himself how he had got caught up in it in the first place.

"Lot of people go around with guns," Elijah said. "What does that prove?"

"Lot of people go around with guns, yes," Virginia said. "I got mine under my pillow right now. But lot of people don't walk the street for nothing with ice all over the ground. Lot of people don't lay up in their room and scream at night. Sunday night he did it again."

"What time Sunday night?" Shepherd asked.

"Do it matter what time?" Virginia asked him.

"We were all drinking together Sunday night," Shepherd said. "He was sitting there with a bunch of us—between eight and nine o'clock."

"He never scream that early, not him," Virginia said. "He likes to wait till everybody's asleep, or fixing to go to sleep, then he starts. I can't see how come he don't do his screaming back there in that graveyard or down that riverbank. I don't know why he's got to bring it here. I don't like it."

"You can put him out," Shepherd said.

"Can I?" Virginia said. "Can I? You and me both know I just can't put him out."

"And why not?"

"If it was that easy, you think I woulda let him in here in the first place?"

"Maybe he'll leave soon," Elijah said.

"No," Virginia said, shaking her head. "He ain't go'n leave soon. He ain't go'n leave soon at all. He come here for something—something we can't do nothing about. And he ain't go'n leave till that thing's done." She looked over her shoulder toward the door. "I knowed that bad weather was go'n bring trouble. Weather like that always bring trouble. I knowed it from the start."

"You're imagining things," Shepherd said.

"Sure," Virginia said, looking up at him. In his face she could see that he believed everything she was saying. "Sure," she said again.

"Let's check upstairs," Elijah said to Shepherd.

They went up to his room and knocked at the door. When he didn't answer, they pushed the door open and went in. The room was extremely cold, the bed unmade, with half of the covers on the floor. Elijah, using just the tips of his fingers, picked up the covers and dropped them on the bed.

"What d'you think?" he asked Shepherd.

Shepherd stood at the window looking down at the alley below. He remembered that Virginia's tenant had described his soul as being much like the alley, cluttered with trash. Elijah came to the window where he was.

"You think Virginia's making sense?" he asked.

"Yes," Shepherd said, and turned from the window. "She's making lot of sense. You didn't see the gun, huh?"

"No," Elijah said.

"Let's get out of here," Shepherd told him.

When they came back downstairs they saw Virginia at her living room door waiting for them.

"Well?" she said.

"He's not up there."

"Thank God for that," she said. "At least he ain't killed himself in there yet. I bet you that room's a mess."

"The bed needs changing," Elijah said.

"Well, I can tell you who ain't go'n change it," Virginia said. "Never catch me in that room all by myself."

"Anybody seen him leave?" Elijah asked.

"If they did they didn't tell me, and I didn't ask nobody," Virginia said.

"When he come back, tell him I was here," Elijah said. "Tell him call the house, and I'll come and pick him up."

"When he show up I'm go'n lock myself in my room," Virginia said. "If y'all want him you better stay here and wait for him yourself. I don't reckon you found that gun?"

"It wasn't up there," Shepherd said.

"It's up there all right," Virginia said. "Just got it hid somewhere till he get good and ready to use it. It wasn't under the pillow, the mattress?"

"We didn't look under there."

"I suppose you think I'm making all this up, too."

"I'm sure you're not making it up, Virginia," Elijah said. "I'll call back later."

He and Shepherd went out on the porch. The cold wind off the St. Charles River whistled through the bare limbs of the pecan tree beside the house. Elijah hunched up his narrow shoulders and rubbed the backs and palms of his hands.

"You don't want drive uptown with me, do you?" he asked Shepherd.

"Drive uptown for what?" Shepherd asked him.

"He might be walking round up there."

"So?"

Elijah gave Shepherd his most sympathetic and helpless look. "It won't take us long," he said.

Shepherd stared at him angrily. He wanted to be with Beverly who was waiting for him at the Congo Room.

"Let's go if we're going," he said, and started down the steps. "And let's make it quick. If I had any sense in my head I'd be with my woman instead of looking for some nut."

They drove uptown, searching both sides of the main street and looking inside the stores, but they couldn't find him anywhere. Virginia had mentioned the riverbank, so Elijah thought he might as well drive along the river for a while. But after going three or four miles out of town, and still finding no sign of him, he turned the car around and started back. Shepherd had given up long ago, and he was becoming more and more irritated.

"One other place," Elijah said. "They've seen him at the Cotton Club on Grant Street."

"What the hell for?" Shepherd asked.

Elijah shrugged his shoulders.

The Cotton Club was the most dilapidated bar in St. Adrienne, and Grant Street wasn't in too much better shape. The street had never been paved, only graveled, and most of the gravel had been washed away, leaving holes in the street a foot deep. The holes were filled with mud and water, and by the time Elijah reached the Cotton Club his car was spattered with mud on all sides. Shepherd went in and asked about Virginia's tenant. The bartender and his one customer were playing checkers at one end of the bar. Neither one had seen him at all that day.

"I guess we ought to just go to the house and wait for him," Elijah said to Shepherd when he got back into the car.

"You can go to the house and wait for him," Shepherd said. "Drop me off at the Congo Room. My woman's waiting for me there."

"What about these two bottles of wine?" Elijah asked.

Shepherd became quite angry. "Listen," he said. "I don't give a damn for that dude. Neither for that damned sherry. I've been doing all this as a favor to you. Now drop me off at the Congo Room. If he show up, give me a buzz, and I might come by. If he don't, save the goddamn wine for some other time. All right?"

Elijah apologized for taking up so much of his time. After dropping him off at the bar, he drove up to Brick O'Linde's grocery store to see if anyone there had seen the tenant. Brick O'Linde behind the counter and the men round the heater all shook their heads. Elijah went back to Virginia's boardinghouse, but Virginia would not even answer the door this time. Elijah couldn't think of anything else to do now but go home. The minister, wearing a dark-brown suit, was waiting out on the porch. He held the screen door open as Elijah came up the walk with the two bottles of wine.

"We couldn't find Robert X," Elijah said.

Phillip looked up the street, then back at Elijah. Elijah could see the disappointment in his face, and now he wished he had searched a little longer.

"The past hour I've been everywhere," he said, and nodded toward the street so Phillip could see the mud on the side of his car.

"What about the others?" Phillip asked him.

"I left them at the Congo Room," Elijah said.

Phillip nodded his head. Elijah could see the hurt in his face. He wanted to stand there with him a moment, but he didn't know what else to say, and he went inside.

The three children, Patrick, Emily, and Joyce Anne, sat in the living room in their school clothes. Phillip had told them not to change clothes, because he wanted them to meet Virginia's new tenant and the teachers when they came to the house.

"Well, where they at?" Patrick asked Elijah.

"They're not coming," Elijah said.

"Good," Patrick said. "Now I can take off these things."

Alma came into the living room wearing a shortsleeved brown wool dress, and a green silk scarf tied round her neck. She had dressed to meet the teachers, but she didn't seem disappointed at all when Elijah told her they weren't coming.

"Where's Phillip?" she asked him.

Elijah nodded over his shoulder. Alma went to the door and looked outside. Phillip had left the porch and was standing out on the lawn looking up the street. Alma started to call him, but changed her mind and turned back to the children.

"All right, you can get out of them clothes now," she said.

She and Elijah exchanged looks. Elijah could tell she was happy that the people were not coming to the house. But he knew that the minister felt just the opposite.

When Phillip came back inside he went directly into his office. He came out for supper and went back in again. He did not take the pills at the table in front of the family, he did not take them at all, he went back into his office and stood at the window. When he got tired standing he sat down at his desk and read from the Bible. At about nine o'clock he came out. He had just crossed the hall to go into the bedroom when he heard a car stop before the house. Elijah and Alma were in the living room, and Elijah got up from the couch to open the door. Phillip looked happy for a moment, but his face suddenly changed when only Shepherd and Beverly came in.

"Sorry to drop by so late," Shepherd said.

"It's still early," Phillip said. "Alma, take their coats."

"No, we just stopped by for a second," Shepherd said, and turned to Elijah. "Afraid I got little bad news for you. Your friend Robert X was picked up by one of Nolan's boys."

Phillip had been standing back, but now he came up closer to Shepherd.

"I was at the Congo Room when I heard Fletcher talking about it," Shepherd said. "He got it from Parlane."

"What they pick him up for?" Phillip asked.

"I don't know," Shepherd said.

"Did he have that gun on him?" Elijah asked Shepherd.

Phillip turned to Elijah. "What gun?"

"According to Virginia, he's got a gun," Elijah said.

"I don't know if he had it or not," Shepherd said. "They picked him up around three this evening. Probably just a few minutes before we started looking for him."

"Where did they pick him up?" Elijah asked.

"Musta been near the bus station for Parlane to see it," Shepherd said.

"I suppose the bus station is closed now?" Phillip asked.

"After that six-thirty bus," Shepherd told him.

"Was Fletcher still at the Congo Room when you left?"

Shepherd nodded. "Yes sir, he was still there."

Phillip turned to Elijah. "Call Thelma," he said. "I don't like this—arresting people for just walking around."

"You think you ought to get in this?" Alma asked him. "Remember Chenal Friday. You probably have to face Nolan then."

"I can't just sit back and let them pick up somebody for walking," Phillip said.

"It had to happen," Shepherd said. "Much as he walk, sooner or later they had to get him."

Elijah had dialed the café and got Fletcher. He passed the telephone to Phillip.

"This is Reverend Martin," he said, speaking calmly into the receiver. He pressed it hard to his ear to hear everything that Fletcher would say to him, but he also pressed it hard to his ear to keep his hand from trembling. He knew the others in the room were watching him and listening to everything he said. He avoided looking at Alma while he spoke. "Yes, I'm fine, I'm fine," he said into the telephone. "Shepherd just told me that this young man at Virginia's place got arrested this evening. You know how I can get in touch with Parlane? You know if he's got a phone?" The others in the room could see him frown as he pressed the telephone to his ear. "No, no, that's all right," he said. "Listen, do you know if he had a gun? Yes, a gun. A pistol. You don't know? You don't think so? All right. Good night. Good night, Fletcher. Thank you kindly."

Phillip hung up the telephone, shaking his head. "Fletcher can sure talk when you get him started," he said, smiling. "I'm sure they just picked him up for walking round up there. I'll call Nolan in the morning."

"Can't this wait till after the meeting Friday?" Alma said. "No matter how the meeting come out you probably go'n have to meet with Nolan then."

"I'll meet him in the morning," Phillip said.

"I hope you know what you doing," Alma told him.

"I know exactly what I'm doing," he said. "Anybody else seen a gun?" he asked Shepherd.

"Elijah and I went in his room and looked around, but we didn't see anything," Shepherd said.

"Virginia's probably making all this up," Phillip said, and smiled. He hoped he was covering up how he truly felt. "Straightening that short hair much as she does done cooked her brains."

"I don't think she's making it up," Shepherd said. "She's scared up there. She thinks he come here to kill somebody. Maybe even himself."

Phillip looked at Shepherd a moment before saying anything. He was still trying to hide his feelings. "You think that's why he's here?"

"I don't know why he's here," Shepherd said. "But I do know he says some strange things. The other day in his room he told me he had cancer of the soul or something. When I asked him what I could do, he said nobody could do nothing." Shepherd shook his head. "I don't know what to think." He turned to Beverly. "Ready to take off, Mama?"

"When you're ready," she said.

"Would y'all like a glass of wine before you go?" Phillip asked. "Got some good sherry there."

"No, thanks," Shepherd said. "We just dropped by for a second."

"I'll walk with you to the car," Phillip said.

"It's a little cold out there," Shepherd said.

"I been there," Phillip told him.

"You ought to put on your overcoat," Alma said.

"I'm just going out there a minute."

She didn't argue with him; she went into the bedroom and came back with his overcoat and his hat. She fastened all the buttons on the coat before she let him leave the room.

"This been some bad weather," Phillip said, looking up at the sky as he followed Shepherd down the walk.

"No sign of letting up either," Shepherd said.

When they came out to the car, Shepherd and Beverly hurried and got inside. Phillip stood beside the car, and Shepherd rolled the glass down to see what else he had to say.

"Drop by again soon," he said. "We still have them two bottles of sherry there."

Shepherd nodded his head. He wanted to leave, but Phillip wouldn't move. He was leaning over into the window now.

"And bring the beautiful Miss Ricord with you," he said.

Beverly smiled at him. But she was as anxious to leave as was Shepherd.

"I used to know a Miss Ricord once," Phillip said to Beverly. "Pretty just like you, Miss Ricord. Not quite as light; hair maybe not quite as long. Pretty just like you. I see you like red; she liked yellow. Wore yellow all the time. Yellow hats, yellow dresses, yellow ribbons. I can't remember the time she didn't have on something yellow."

Beverly could see how serious he was, and she smiled patiently at him.

"What happened?" Shepherd asked.

"I lost her," Phillip said.

"Somebody took her from you?"

Phillip shook his head. "Nobody could ever do that."

"How did you lose her?"

Phillip looked at Shepherd as though he might tell him about it, then he changed his mind. It was too complicated to talk about while leaning into the window of a car. It was something you couldn't talk about to two people who were anxious to leave. He looked at both of them, remembering when it was he and Johanna who wanted to get away and be alone.

"Some other time," he said. "Promise me you'll come back soon."

"A promise," Beverly said, and smiled at him again.

Phillip stood back from the car and Shepherd drove away. When he could no longer see the red taillights of the car, he went back into the yard.

The next morning he drove uptown to get his son out of jail. Walking across the sea-shell-covered parking lot he heard the big clock on the courthouse steeple strike twice for nine thirty. On his left, as he turned up the walk to go inside, was the statue of the Confederate soldier standing at parade rest. Six or seven feet above the head of the statue, fluttering calmly in the cool morning air, were the state, national, and Confederate flags. Phillip Martin took off his hat as he mounted the first step.

The sheriff's office was at the far end of the hall, and Phillip took a deep breath before entering the room. A young deputy dressed in a light-blue uniform sat at a front desk looking through papers. Another deputy sitting at a desk in the back of the room was trying desperately to type fast using only two fingers. The first deputy knew that Phillip had come in, but he let him stand there a while before looking up.

"Help you, Reverend?" he asked.

"Sheriff Nolan in?"

"Yeah. But he's busy. Can I help you?"

"I would like to see Nolan."

"You'll have to wait."

The deputy started looking through his papers again. After Phillip had been standing there about five minutes, the deputy got up from his desk and went into another room. When he came back out he looked through his papers another minute or two before saying anything.

"You can go in," he said, without looking up.

Nolan was sitting behind his desk reading a newspaper when Phillip came into the room. Nolan was a tall, slim, well-built man in his late fifties. His hair was the color of dry corn shuck, except at the temples and the sideburns, which were almost white. Nolan and Phillip were not too far apart in age and they had known each other most of their lives. As a young deputy Nolan had arrested Phillip several times for fighting. Twice he had been picked up as a suspect in killings, but neither time was there enough proof against him. As the sheriff of St. Adrienne, Nolan had arrested him more than once for civil rights demonstrations. The two men had no love for each other, still there was no running hatred for each other either. Each felt the other was doing his work the best way he knew how, and both accepted the fact that there would be conflicts between them.

Nolan folded his papers and laid them on the desk and nodded for Phillip to sit down. Phillip hesitated a moment, then he moved back to the chair. He spun his hat on his fingers a couple times while Nolan sat there watching him.

"Well?" Nolan said.

"I heard you arrested a young man yesterday," Phillip said.

"We picked up somebody yesterday—yes," Nolan said.

"Can you tell me what for?"

"Why?" Nolan asked.

"I want to bail him out."

"Did he call for you?"

"No."

"Then why?"

"I know his people."

Nolan watched him. "Yes?" he said.

Phillip passed his hand over the sweatband of the hat. He didn't feel comfortable, and he knew Nolan saw it.

"How much is bail?" Phillip asked.

"Hold your horses," Nolan said. "Who are these people?"

"Just some people I know."

"Yes?" Nolan said. "Where from?"

"Chicago," Phillip said, avoiding his eyes.

"Chicago?" Nolan said, watching him.

Phillip rubbed his finger round the sweatband of the hat again.

"All right," Nolan said. "What is it?"

"What is what?" Phillip asked.

"Between you and that boy?" Nolan said. "I think that's what we're talking about."

"I just told you," Phillip said.

"That's not it, 'less you think I'm a fool," Nolan said. "I want to know exactly what he means to you."

Phillip held the expensive black felt hat in his left hand while caressing it nervously with his fingers. Nolan was watching him, and he felt more and more uncomfortable. He drew in a deep breath and exhaled through his mouth.

"My son," he said.

"Come again?"

"My son," he said, looking at Nolan.

"You pulling my leg?" Nolan asked.

"You knew his mother," Phillip said. "Johanna Rey. Reno Plantation."

"Johanna? Johanna? Johanna?" Nolan said, thinking.

"They left from here about twenty years ago," Phillip said. "Maybe little—"

"Rey? Rey? Rey?" Nolan went on. "Yes, I recall Reys

there at Reno. Yes. The old one, the mama, didn't she cook for Dr. Morgan there for years?"

"For years," Phillip said.

Nolan nodded his head. He looked at Phillip, grinning. "Well, well," he said. "Scratch my back and call me Kelly."

He got up from the desk and went to the water jug in the corner of the room. Phillip heard the water bubbling as Nolan filled the paper cup. After drinking, he dropped the cup into the wastepaper basket and came back to his desk.

"Yes sir, scratch my back and call me Kelly," he said again.

He was watching Phillip, and Phillip was looking past him toward the wooden lattice behind the windowpanes. He wasn't feeling well at all. Maybe he had made a mistake coming here like this. Maybe he should have talked with his attorney, Anthony McVay. Anthony could have gotten the boy out of here without any problems, and he probably would have paid much less bail.

"Let's start all over," Nolan said. "Let's start with why he's staying at Virginia's and not with you. Look to me like he ought to be in his father's house."

"I suppose that's how it ought to be," Phillip said.

"Well?"

"He's been there once," Phillip said.

"But he's not staying there? Why? No room?"

"I could make room, if that was all."

"Then why isn't he there?" Nolan asked.

"I don't know."

"What you mean you don't know? Haven't you asked him?"

"I haven't said a word to him."

Nolan leaned forward on the desk and squinted at Phillip.

"What the hell is going on round here?" he asked. "You taking me for a damn fool or something?"

"I'm telling you the truth," Phillip said. "I ain't said a

word to him—not one. That's why I'm here to get him out—so we can talk."

Nolan didn't know whether to believe Phillip or not. He sat back in the chair and watched him a moment. Phillip had begun sweating.

"Let's start all over," Nolan said. "Y'all ain't talked, y'all ain't seen each other in over twenty years—and he had to be a little nothing when he left from here—how you know he's your son?"

"I know my blood," Phillip said.

"Your blood?"

"My blood."

"I see," Nolan said, squinting from behind the desk at Phillip. "Your blood."

"How much is it?" Phillip asked.

"Depends on what I have on my hand," Nolan said. "He might be a killer. Might be a rapist—though I don't think he's got the strength for that. But he could be a thief. Draft-dodger? Psycho? He could be almost anything. No papers. See, I don't know what I have on my hand."

"He's my son," Phillip said. "And he come here to see me." He started to tell Nolan about the dream, but he thought it was best to keep this to himself. "We just haven't had a chance to talk yet," he said. "He's no killer, no rapist—nothing like that. Just my son."

Nolan nodded his head. "Just your son?"

"Yes," Phillip said. "My son."

"How do you know he wants to go with you?" Nolan asked. "According to you, y'all ain't said a word to each other in the week he's been here—how you know he wants to say something to you now?"

"I think he rather be with me than in here."

"I ain't too sure of that," Nolan said. "I done picked up many who rather stay in jail. We'll ask him." He looked at the door. "Sidney?"

The deputy opened the door and came in.

"Go open Jenkin cell, bring me that boy out of there."

The deputy left. Nolan looked at Phillip.

"If he want to go, I'll set bail."

"I'll pay anything," Phillip said.

Nolan grinned. "Trying to bribe me, Phillip?" he asked.

"I just want my son."

"I don't think he is your son," Nolan said. "I heard you fell the other day—been working too hard. You getting up there in age, old fellow. How old are you now?"

"Couple years older than you."

"That's why I take it easy," Nolan said. "You ought to do the same. Slow up."

"My falling didn't have nothing to do with being tired," Phillip said. "I'm in good shape."

"Not according to Cecil LeBeau," Nolan said. "Not according to Octave Bacheron."

Phillip reached into his inside coat pocket to get his checkbook. "How much?" he asked again.

"Still think he's your son, not just your mind playing tricks, huh?"

"He's my son," Phillip said. "How much?"

"All depends on whether he wants to go."

"He'll have to go if you tell him to go."

"Want him that bad, huh?"

"Yes," Phillip said. He had already taken out the checkbook. Now he was reaching for his pen.

"He's yours," Nolan said.

"How much?"

"No money."

Phillip had already opened the checkbook to start writing, but now he stopped, the pen still poised.

"Don't bother Chenal," Nolan said.

"What do you mean?"

"Just don't go up there Friday."

"I have to go to Chenal Friday," Phillip said.

"Don't," Nolan said.

"What about those people out there?"

"That's your problem."

"No, this is my problem in here," Phillip said. "I'm willing to pay money for my problem in here. I can't take from them people what they been working for for so long. We just about changed everything in this town—except Chenal. He's the only one still holding out, the only one won't go along. I can't do that to my people."

"Maybe you don't want the boy much as you think you do," Nolan said. "Well?"

Phillip began trembling. Not so much from anger as from total disbelief of what he was hearing from Nolan.

"We always been straight with each other," he said. "We always had problems—in our business we go'n have problems—but we always handled it like men."

"True," Nolan said, nodding his head.

"Then why this?"

"You asking a favor," Nolan said. "I'm offering a favor for a favor. This weather is too bad for a man my age, or your age, too, to be out there."

"I have money here," Phillip said, showing him the checkbook.

"I know you have money," Nolan said. "The rich give you money and expensive jewelry. Look at your wrist, look at your fingers. The poor, they give you whatever they can scrape up. I know all about your money."

"I have a right to bail him out," Phillip said.

"I have some rights too, Phillip," Nolan said. "I have the right to hold a suspicious character."

"Suspicious of what?"

"I'll find something," Nolan said. "No papers, no home address, no job—loitering. He could be a psycho. He looks a little off."

"I can always get my lawyer," Phillip said.

Nolan wanted to grin, but he didn't. Neither did he say

anything; he just nodded toward the telephone. Phillip didn't look at it.

"That's right," Nolan said. "This personal, not political. They can't blow it up like they can do a demonstration. Go on, call him and see. See what he cares about blood kin. The only time they care about blood is when it's running in the street. They don't give a damn for your kin. Try him. Go on, call him."

The deputy pushed the door open to come into the room, but Nolan waved him back.

"Well?" he said to Phillip. "You want him or not?"

"Can I have some water?" Phillip asked.

"Jug's over there," Nolan said, nodding his head. "Help yourself."

While Phillip was at the water jug, Nolan picked up the newspapers and propped his feet on the desk again. Phillip drank two cups of water and came back to the chair. He started to sit down, but he changed his mind. He stood before the desk with his hat in his hand. Nolan was still reading the papers, his feet still on the desk.

"I can't do that to my people," Phillip said.

"It's up to you," Nolan said. "I'll tell Sidney to take him back."

"Can't I even talk to him?"

"No."

Phillip stared down at Nolan, shaking his head.

"Why you doing this to me?" he asked. "Why you persecuting me?"

Nolan let his feet slide away from the desk as he folded the papers and laid them aside. He had controlled himself long as he could.

"Persecuting you?" he said. "Persecuting you how?"

"You know this all they have out there," Phillip said. "What else do they have?"

"That whole damn thing is over with," Nolan said.

"Over with. When they nailed that coffin down on King, that demonstrating was over with. All you doing now is bullshitting the people, that's all. It's over with."

"Maybe for the young," Phillip said. "But the old—that's all they have."

"They better find something else," Nolan said. "That bullshit's over with. Well, you want him or not? I don't have all day."

"I won't be able to stop the people," Phillip said.

"No?" Nolan said. "Sidney?" he called.

The deputy pushed the door open.

"Take that boy back to that cell—and lock it."

"Wait," Phillip said. "Can't I speak to him just one second?"

"No," Nolan said.

The deputy pulled the door shut.

"Wait," Phillip said.

The deputy stood in the outer room with his hand on the door knob. Nolan sat behind his desk looking up at Phillip, waiting.

"You won't take money?" Phillip asked again.

"I think I made myself clear," Nolan said. "You want him, or you don't want him?"

Phillip looked down at Nolan and nodded his head.

"I always thought you was different," he said. "Just go to show how wrong a man can be."

7

The deputy pushed the door open, and Phillip's heart started racing as he watched his son come into the room. He wore the big overcoat unfastened and the cap stuffed down into one of the pockets. His thin, patchy beard was as nappy as the hair on his head. Phillip reached his hand out toward him, but he went by as if Phillip was not even there. Nolan, who had been watching both of them, was trying to find some kind of resemblance between the two, but he could find nothing.

"Reverend here paid a lot to get you out," he said. "Claims you his son. Well?"

"I don't know," the boy answered him. He was standing directly in front of Nolan, but he spoke so quietly that even Nolan could hardly hear him.

"Well, I reckon you got a point there," Nolan said. "Something none of us can be sure of. What's your name, boy?"

"Robert X."

"In here, boy, you say 'yes sir' and 'no sir,' " Nolan said.

"Robert X—sir."

"Before it was X?" Nolan asked him.

"I went by my mother's name." He spoke quietly, unemotionally, looking down at the desk and not at Nolan.

"Her name?" Nolan asked.

"Sims."

"Sims?"

"Yes sir. Sims," he said, nodding his head.

"Not Rey? Not Martin?"

He shook his head this time. "Sims—sir."

Nolan looked at Phillip. "You never married her, did you?" But he knew Phillip had not married the woman, and he didn't wait for an answer. He turned back to the boy before him.

"What you doing here, Sims—X—whatever you call yourself?"

"I like to be addressed as Robert X, sir," he said, looking at Nolan for the first time. It was not a demand, he was merely emphasizing that Robert X was his only name.

"What you doing here, Robert X?" Nolan asked, after looking him over a moment. He had searched his face for defiance, he wanted defiance, but he found none. Not only did the boy's face not show emotion, he seemed incapable of having any.

"I'm on my way to a conference," he said. "Sir."

"I didn't hear 'bout no conference here in St. Adrienne."

"I'm here to meet a man."

"This the man?" Nolan asked, nodding toward Phillip.

The boy didn't turn his head.

"A man," he said, looking only at Nolan.

"I see," Nolan said. "You know, Sims—Robert X—we got ways of making people talk. I've cracked tougher nuts than you."

The boy looked down at him without answering. Nolan still searched his face for defiance but couldn't find any.

"Well," he said, "you not my problem any more, you his now. Just make sure you stay on the other side of them tracks. I don't want have to pick you up again—we understand each other?"

"Yes sir."

Nolan jerked his head toward the door.

"Wait out there."

The boy turned away from the desk without ever looking at Phillip and left the room.

"Well?" Nolan said. "You still want him?"

"He's my son."

"He sure don't look like you," Nolan said. "You sure you didn't hit your head when you fell?"

"I ought to know my blood," Phillip said.

"Well, keep your blood back there long as you want him, then put him on the first thing smoking. I don't want him in this town."

"Anybody else have to know about this?" Phillip asked.

"They'll have to know before Friday," Nolan said.

"Let me tell them my way."

"Sure," Nolan said. "Long as they don't come up here starting trouble. It's too cold to go out there arresting people. Especially old people who ought to be home by the fire. We understand each other, Phillip?"

Phillip looked down at him and nodded his head. "We understand each other, Sheriff. We understand each other well."

"Good," Nolan said, and picked up his papers. "Long as we understand each other."

When Phillip came into the outer room he saw the boy standing by the front desk. The two deputies went on with their work as if nothing was going on round them. The deputy at the front desk was still looking through papers, just as he was doing when Phillip first came in. The one in back was still typing with two fingers. Phillip nodded for the boy to leave and followed him out into the hall.

"They treat you all right?" he asked.

The boy pulled the cap out of the coat pocket and put it on his head. He didn't bother to answer.

"I want us to go for a ride," Phillip said. "I want us to talk."

The cool air off the St. Charles River hit them as they came outside. They passed by the statue of the Confederate soldier and the three flags and walked across the sea-shell-covered parking lot over to the car.

"We can get something to eat if you want," Phillip said. "We can pick up a box lunch and—"

But there was no point going on, because the boy wasn't listening to him. He opened the door for him to get into the car, then he went round to the other side. He drove out of St. Adrienne without knowing or caring where he was going. On his left was the St. Charles River, high, muddy, and gray, the waves flowing far upon the bank, splashing against the trunks of the cypress and willow trees before receding back into the river again. The small, black *poules d'eau* floating lightly, effortlessly, on the high waves would duck under in search of food, then bob up some fifteen or twenty feet away. They would look around jerkily for a couple of seconds and go back down again. On the other side of the road were the gray unpainted farmhouses and an occasional antebellum Creole house sitting on blocks seven or eight feet above the ground. Pecan, live-oak, and cypress trees grew in many of the yards, as well as alongside the road, and sometimes the Spanish moss hung so low overhead you could almost reach out and touch it.

Since leaving St. Adrienne, Phillip had been trying to think of a way to start a conversation with his son. Then he caught him looking out at the houses on his side of the road.

"Them old houses you see there, they been there for years and years," he told him. "You know why they built them up like that?"

He didn't get an answer.

"Years, years ago, water used to cover everything," he

went on. "So they had to put the houses high up on blocks to keep out the water. Today we got the spillways, thank God; you can build your house any way you want."

But now that he had mentioned the houses, the boy, whom he could never call Robert X, had no more interest in them and turned his head.

Phillip drove about five miles along the river, then he turned off the highway onto a narrow blacktop road that led them into the canefields. The cane had been cut, hauled away, the leaves had been burned off, leaving the ground black from the fire. On either side of the road, about a quarter of a mile away, was the beginning of the swamps. The trees from this distance looked like an impenetrable black wall bordering the fields.

Phillip drove another couple of miles, then parked the car near a large old oak tree beside the road. The limbs of the tree, thick with leaves and heavily laden with Spanish moss, hung all the way over the road into the other field. Not a house was in sight from here, and no one could be seen in the fields either, so Phillip thought this was a good place to sit and talk. But after sitting there a while, fumbling with his hands and watching the boy, he still didn't know where or how to begin.

The boy hadn't said a word since leaving the sheriff's office. He sat as far away from Phillip as he could and stared out at the tree just ahead of the car. Phillip could see the nervous thumping of the jaw muscles underneath the scraggly beard.

"How's your mother?" he finally asked. "Is she all right?"

"She's not all right," the boy answered quietly, without looking round.

"What's the matter?" Phillip asked.

"Grieving herself to death."

"Grieving?" Phillip asked. "Grieving over what?"

"Her two children."

"Something happened to the children?"

The boy nodded his head, as he stared out at the tree in front of the car. "Something happened to the children," he said quietly, thoughtfully.

Phillip waited for him to go on, but he didn't.

"What happened?" Phillip asked.

Instead of answering, the boy turned to look at him. His face didn't show hatred, at least the eyes didn't show it, they showed pain. But Phillip could feel the hatred there. He felt it strongly and quickly as he would have felt a blow with a club, or a cut with a knife. They stared at each other a moment, then he saw the boy's eyes shifting to his clothes—hat, coat, trousers—as if he might be comparing them to his own. When the boy looked back at him again, the eyes showed no more hatred than before, but Phillip knew it was there.

"You interested?" he asked.

Phillip had forgotten what he had asked him, but he nodded his head anyway.

"They both dead," the boy said calmly.

"Dead?" he asked, and bit into his bottom lip.

" 'Leven years," the boy said. His face calm as his voice. Still, Phillip could feel the hatred there.

"Why I'm just hearing 'bout it?" he asked.

"We didn't know you was interested."

"Not interested in my own flesh and blood?"

"You never showed no interest in your own flesh and blood before. We didn't know if you be interested in your own flesh and blood then."

Phillip bit into his bottom lip as he studied the thin, bearded face. He knew the boy hated him, and he wasn't sure he could believe what he was telling him now.

"If this happened that long back, what bringing you here now?"

"Revenge," the boy said directly, yet calmly, his face showing no more emotion than it would have shown if he had looked out at the fields. "Revenge," he repeated.

"Revenge?" Phillip asked him. "Revenge for what?"

"For destroying me. For making me the eunuch I am. For destroying my family: my mama, my brother, my sister."

"How did I destroy you, destroy the family?" Phillip asked him. "I ain't seen one of y'all in twenty years—over twenty years. How did I destroy you?"

The boy grunted and started to turn away, but Phillip grabbed his arm. The boy looked down at the hand a moment, then pried it loose and slammed it back.

"You my son," Phillip said. "I have my rights. I can touch you if I want."

"I'm a moment of your lust," the boy said.

"You my son, no matter what," Phillip said. "No matter what happened, you still my son."

"I'm a moment of your lust," the boy repeated.

"Johanna know you here?"

"She gived me the money."

"You lying," Phillip said. "You lying."

The boy turned away. He was quiet a moment as he stared out at the tree in front of the car.

"Yes, she gived me the money," he said. "When I heard where you was, I told her I wanted to come here and kill you for destroying the family. And she slapped me. She slapped me so hard I went blind. She went and got the jar of money and slammed it down on the floor in front of me. She made me get down there and pick up every penny. I cut my hands, I cut my knees, picking up pennies and wrinkled old dollar bills." He turned back to Phillip again, his eyes showing more pain than hatred. " 'Get yourself a ticket and go kill him,' she told me. 'Sew back your nuts by killing your father.' But I can't sew them back by killing you, can I? Can I, *Father*?"

Phillip looked horrified. He didn't know what was going on. He looked around as if he were looking for someone to help him. But no one else was there, and he turned back to his son.

"Boy, what are you talking about? What are you saying?"

"It's not boy, Father. It's Robert X."

"It's not Robert X," Phillip said. "It's not even Robert."

"Then what is it, Father?"

"I don't know," Phillip said. "I don't know yours, I don't know your brother's, I don't know your sister's. But you mine, and I love you. I love you now, and I loved you then. I was too weak then to do anything. Today I have strength. 'Cause today I have God."

The boy looked at him and grinned. Then he laughed. He looked at Phillip's expensive clothes, laughing. He looked at the jewelry on his hands, laughing. He looked back in his face, he just couldn't stop laughing.

"That's what the man told Mama," he said. "Told Mama you had found God, and you was down here saving souls. Mama thought it was the funniest thing she'd ever heard. You down here saving souls. After you had destroyed us, you down here saving souls. Don't you think that's funny? I think it's funny. Mama thought it was funny."

Phillip shook his head. His eyes had suddenly filled with tears. "I didn't destroy you, boy."

"Robert X, Father," he said. He wasn't laughing any more. And he wasn't suppressing his hatred any more either. His face quivered, his nostrils expanded, the hatred in his eyes went deep into Phillip's heart. "If you didn't destroy me, who did?"

"That world out there."

"The world?"

"The world."

"The world laid with her in the field?" the boy asked him. "Where did you take her? In the ditch? Between the cane rows? In the weeds near the swamps? Where at, *Father*?"

Phillip bit into his lips, the tears running down his face.

"Now you put it on the world," the boy said, taunting

him more now that he was crying. "Did the world push them three dollars in my hand that day? That was twenty-one years ago, but I can still see them, feel them, smell them. Even after she made me bring them back to you I could still smell the stink in my hand. Three dollars. A dollar for each one of us. That's what you paid. A dollar for each one of us."

Phillip was still crying. But he clenched his fist. "I won't allow that," he said. "I won't allow you to talk about her like that. I won't allow it."

"I'm not talking about her, I'm talking about you. You treated her like a common whore. I held the three dollars in my hand. I, I, I held them. I had to carry the money to the wagon, and take it back. I had to do it."

"That's all I had in the world," Phillip said. "I didn't even own myself then. Nothing. Nothing else but the rags on my back. But you wrong when you say I treated her like a whore. I loved your mother, your mother loved me. Yes, we loved in the fields. But the fields was not dirty. The fields was clean. Clean as any bed."

"You mean your lust couldn't wait till you got to bed."

Phillip trembled with anger. It was hard to control his voice as well as his urge to hit him. "I loved her," he said. "I loved her, and she loved me. That's why she slapped you, boy. That's why she slapped you."

"She slapped me because she loved you, and she still love you. But you never loved her, or us. You raped her. You tried to pay off with three dollars."

"I never raped nobody," Phillip said. "Surely not her. I gived you three dollars 'cause that's all I had."

"You had more," the boy said. "You had a mouth, a voice. You had arms, you had legs. You coulda walked out that door. That's all she wanted. You to walk out that door and call her back. That's all she wanted."

"You just don't understand," Phillip said. He was not trying to control the tears that rolled down his face. Neither was he trying to control his voice now, it was choked with emotion. "I couldn't bit more leave that room, that woman I didn't care nothing in the world for, than I can right now carry this car here on my back. I was paralyzed. Paralyzed. Yes, I had a mouth, but I didn't have a voice. I had legs, but I couldn't move. I had arms, but I couldn't lift them up to you. It took a man to do these things, and I wasn't a man. I was just some other brutish animal who could cheat, steal, rob, kill—but not stand. Not be responsible. Not protect you or your mother. They had branded that in us from the time of slavery. That's what kept me on that bed. Not 'cause I didn't want to get up. I wanted to get up more than anything in the world. But I had to break the rules, rules we had lived by for so long, and I wasn't strong enough to break them then."

He stopped and looked at his son. The boy's face was turned from him. Phillip's hand went out to touch him but stopped inches away from the sleeve of the coat.

"I'm a man today. I prayed for Him to make me a man, and He made me a man. I can stand today. I have a voice today." He stopped again. "You listening to anything I'm saying to you?" he asked.

"He answers fathers' prayers," the boy said without looking around. "Not sons'."

"All men's prayers."

"Not all men's," he said, turning to look at Phillip, his eyes painfully sad. "Not all men's. I prayed, and prayed, and prayed. He never answered mine. I know He never answered mine."

"What happened back there?" Phillip asked him.

The boy raised his hand up to his temple as if he was in pain, and Phillip could see by his eyes that his mind was wandering.

"What happened?" Phillip asked again.

"My sister viciously raped," he said. "Viciously raped. Instead of me taking the gun like I shoulda done, I took her in my arms and called on God. Viciously raped, her young body torn and bloody—and I sat there rocking her in my arms, crying, and calling on God."

Phillip's chest suddenly seemed very full, and he raised his hand and rubbed it hard. Twice he tried to speak, but neither time could he make a sound.

"My brother brought the gun to me," the boy went on. "Pushed it on me three times. 'Go kill that dog. Go kill that dog.' But all I did was sit there holding my sister and crying. So he did it for me. He found the man, shooting pool, and blew out his brains."

Phillip covered his mouth with his hand to keep from crying.

"Every day of my life I regret I didn't kill him myself. Every day of my life since that day. Every day."

"No," Phillip said. "No. That's what the law is for. That's what the law's there for."

"Law?" the boy asked, as if the word was foreign to him. "There ain't no law. Why should the law protect us when the father won't? You think the law should care more for the family than the father? By law she wasn't even raped. Black girls don't get raped, black girls entice their rapist. Like Mama musta enticed you."

"What happened to your brother?" Phillip asked.

"What you think happens to a black boy when he kills? The law takes charge."

"They killed him?"

"For all we're concerned, they killed him. He didn't want nothing to do with me or Mama when he came out of that prison."

"Why your mother?"

" 'Cause it was her man who raped my sister."

"How can I get in touch with Johanna, with my other two children?" Phillip asked.

"I don't know how to get in touch with my brother and sister myself," the boy said. "And even if I did and told you it wouldn't do any good. They don't know you exist. They don't know you ever did."

"I don't believe this," Phillip said, shaking his head and biting into his lip.

"Why not?"

"I am their father," he said. "No matter what."

"Not to them," the boy said. "They wiped you out of their minds the day they left that plantation. The way you wipe all the letters and numbers off a blackboard. No father, no more than there's God or law."

"There's father," Phillip said. "There's God and law. Always was. Always will be."

"Not to them. Not to me no more either."

"I'm father," Phillip said. "No matter what. I'm father. To you and to them."

The boy looked at him a long time. The face showed more pain, more hurt, than hatred.

"Say my name," he said. "Don't call me boy no more, Father. Say my name."

Phillip could not. The boy grunted to himself and turned to get out of the car. Phillip grabbed his coat sleeve.

"Where you going?" he asked.

"For a walk. For a good long walk."

"It's ten miles back to St. Adrienne. And it's cold out there."

"I been cold before."

He pulled himself free and got out of the car. Phillip got out on his side and came round the front of the car to meet him.

"You in my charge still," he said. "And I want you at my house."

"I'm not going to your house," the boy told him.

"You rather be in that jail?"

"I'm not going back there either," he said. "I'm going for a walk."

He looked across the fields toward the swamps. The

trees looked like an impenetrable black wall from this distance.

"You need money?" Phillip asked.

"No."

"You got any?"

"I don't have none, and I don't need none," the boy said. "I don't need nothing from you any more."

He started to walk away.

"Wait," Phillip said. "Wait. You didn't live too far from here. Let's go over to the old place. Visit your nanane. She christened both of us—me and you. She'll be glad to see you, I'm sure."

The boy walked off again.

"Wait, wait, wait," Phillip said. This time he got in front of him. But he didn't ask it. He couldn't bring himself to ask it. Still he knew the boy knew what he wanted. "You wouldn't deny me that?" he said.

The boy looked at him and walked away. Phillip watched him go farther and farther across the fields. When his coat became the same color as the trees, Phillip turned, his head down, and went back to the car.

After sitting there quietly a moment, he started out for Reno Plantation. He would travel the blacktop road a short distance, then a graveled road would take him the last seven or eight miles. He knew this road as he knew his hand, but when he reached Reno Plantation he couldn't recall having seen a thing. He knew he had passed the store and post office at McCabe. He knew he had crossed the wooden bridge at the Two Indians Bayou near Hobson, and that the road had made a sharp V-like turn to the left. He had passed the old church at Silas Woods where he had gone to grammar school. He had passed many, many houses, and he had probably passed a lot of people who waved at him. He had crossed the railroad tracks at Shottsville, and he had driven past the old weighing scale and the old wooden derrick. He had to have passed all these things to get here, but he couldn't recall any of it. He was not aware of place or time until he reached the quarters of Reno Plantation. Driving down the thinly graveled muddy road, he looked out at the few old unpainted houses still there. The house where he had lived was torn down, and the one where Johanna and the children had lived was also gone. Now weeds and shrubbery had taken over where houses, yards, and vegetable gardens had been.

Phillip stopped the car in front of his godmother's house, but now he was ashamed to go inside. How could he go in there and tell her how he felt? What would she think of him if he went in there and told her what had happened only a few miles away from here? But if he couldn't go to her, where else could he go? Back to St. Adrienne and stand at the window again?

He sat in the car looking into the yard at the house. The yard was clean and bare, except for a mulberry tree on the left side of the walk and a rose bush on either side of the steps. The house itself was exactly like every other one in the quarters. They all had the same rusted corrugated tin roofs with a brick chimney sitting in the center. They all had the same long, warped porches, with three or four steps leading up to the porch. Every house had two doors facing the road. All had been whitewashed at the same time, twenty-five or thirty years ago—none had been painted since—and the weather had turned all of them the same ashy gray color.

Phillip thought about driving away before anyone saw him, but he was sure somebody had looked out of a door and seen him already. Maybe even his nanane knew he was sitting out there watching the house.

He thought he heard someone chopping wood in the back yard, and he rolled down the glass to listen better. He could hear the axe louder now, and he could hear men talking and laughing. He looked up at the chimney, and he could see a trickle of blue smoke rising above the roof and drifting down the quarters. Why hadn't she gotten a gas heater like most of the other people were doing? He had begged her to get one. He had even tried to buy her one. But she told him if he brought it there she wouldn't even let it inside the house.

"What I want a heater for?" she asked. "Wood made to burn, ain't it? What you go'n do with wood if you don't burn it, hanh? Eat it?"

He got out of the car and went up to the house and knocked.

"Come in," his godmother called from inside.

He pushed the door open and went into a dark room that smelled of salt pork and cabbage. There was a fire in the fireplace but no other light, and it took him a while to get accustomed to the darkness. He saw his godmother, Angelina Bouie, sitting in a rocking chair at one end of the fireplace. She wore a headrag, she had on a sweater over her dress, and she had a small blanket over her legs to keep the fire from scorching them. Loretta Williams, a much larger woman and a few years younger than Angelina, sat at the other end of the fireplace. A heavy topcoat and a man's felt hat hung on the back of her chair. Both Loretta and Angelina were eating peanuts and throwing the shells into the fire.

"I do declare," Loretta said.

"It's about time you showed up here," Angelina said. "You done forgot I'm still alive, Phillip?"

"No, Nanane," he said. After taking off his hat and coat and laying them on the bed by the door, he came to the fireplace and kissed Angelina on the forehead. He spoke to Loretta, then he sat down in one of the chairs between them.

"How've you been, Nanane?"

"Don't look like it matter to you much."

He smiled at her. She would complain whether he came here once a day or once a year.

"I hear you fell," she said.

"That sure gets around."

"What you doing falling, Phillip?" she asked him.

"I don't know. Tired," he said.

"Tired?" she said. "Somebody big and strong like you tired enough to go round here falling?"

Phillip turned to the other woman.

"How are you, Sis Williams?" he asked her.

"Fine. Yourself?"

"I'm feeling better," he said.

"What brought you out here in weather like this?" Angelina asked him from the other side. "Don't tell me you come all the way from St. Adrienne just to see me?"

"I did," he said, opening out his hands toward the fire.

"I know better," Angelina said. "You want some of these goobers? Hand him some of them goobers there, Lo-re-ta."

Loretta Williams gave Phillip a handful of peanuts out of an aluminum bread pan that she had on the floor by her chair. The peanuts had been roasted in the hot ashes in the fireplace.

"Somebody cutting wood in the back?" Phillip asked.

"Louis and them cutting me some wood," Angelina said. "You don't never come out here."

"You ought to get a heater," he told her.

"I don't want no heater," she said. "And I don't like the way you looking neither. You don't look right. Look at him there, Lo-re-ta. He still don't look right. That gal still don't know how to look after you, Phillip, after all these years?"

"Alma is my wife, Nanane, and she knows how to look after me," Phillip said. "She's got nothing to do with how I look."

"Lean over here, let me feel your forrid," Angelina said.

"I'm all right, Nanane."

"Feel his forrid for me there, Lo-re-ta."

Loretta Williams got up heavily and placed the palm of a dry, well-callused hand against Phillip's forehead.

"Hot all right," she said.

"It's that fire," Phillip said.

"Can be," Loretta said, and moved back to her chair.

Phillip broke open the shells with his thumb and forefinger, and ate the peanuts while staring into the fire. He knew that his godmother was still watching him, and he was glad the other woman was there.

"Phillip, anything going on in St. Adrienne you don't want me to know about?" Angelina asked him.

"Nothing's going on," he said, looking into the fire and not at her.

"Some of them Cajuns been threatening you again, Phillip?"

"Cajuns?" he said, looking at her.

"Cajuns. Sure—Cajuns. You don't know what a Cajun is?"

"No, nobody been threatening me, Nanane," he said.

"Then how come you didn't call me when you fell?"

"You don't have a telephone, Nanane."

"Lisa got a phone there."

"Lisa live a mile from here."

"She got them children. Can't they walk?"

He looked at the small, very old woman sitting back in the chair with the blanket spread over her legs. He loved her very much, and he wished he could tell her everything. But just as he had been unable to say it to anyone else, he couldn't say it to her either.

"I'm sitting up in my house, and Louis come here telling me you done fell. I'm here waiting and waiting for some kind of news—nothing. Not a word. I woulda come there myself, wasn't for my rheumatism acting up."

Phillip had turned from her and was looking down at the fire again.

"Now you come here in all this bad weather," she went on. "Look at me when I talk to you, Phillip. I ain't just talking for my good health."

He looked at her.

"You don't want talk in front of Lo-re-ta there? You

want her to go stand in the kitchen? It got fire in that stove, it's warm back there."

"I don't mind," Loretta said.

"Keep your seat, Sis Williams," Phillip said. He turned back to his godmother. "There's nothing to talk about, Nanane. I just came out here because I wanted to see you."

She continued to watch him. She was still eating the peanuts, chewing them only with her front teeth, which were brown and crooked.

"Have it your own way," she said. "I'm coming to St. Adrienne soon as I can get around. Something ain't right in St. Adrienne, and I 'tend to find out what it is."

He turned from her and looked down at the fire again. To his right, Loretta Williams sat talking to herself. "Goobers ain't what they used to be. Nothing inside these shells." She cracked open the peanut shells louder than either Phillip or Angelina did, and Phillip thought she was doing this purposely, since she was not in the conversation.

Phillip could hear the men laughing and talking while they chopped wood behind the house. He would have liked to go out there and take his turn with the axe. It had been like that once—years ago. He and other young men had gone from house to house to help out each other. It was always easier and more fun than working alone. Together they could laugh and talk. The work was never too hard, and the weather was never too cold. Reckless years. Not caring years. Only fun-loving years.

He had quit eating the peanuts now, and he was staring in the fire and shaking his head.

"Phillip, what's wrong with you?" Angelina asked. "Phillip?"

He turned to her. "I was dreaming. You said something, Nanane?"

She looked at him a while without saying anything. She wanted him to know that when she was talking she wanted his undivided attention. She also wanted him to know that she believed there was something wrong in St. Adrienne.

"I said, Chippo saw Johanna."

"Chippo?" he said. For a moment it didn't mean anything, because he was still half dreaming. Even when he heard her mentioning Johanna's name, he thought it was just his mind playing tricks. But then he remembered that the boy had said something about a man coming to the house. And he remembered that while Chippo was in the Merchant Marine he used to ship out to sea from the West Coast. "Chippo?" he said. "Chippo?"

"Yes. Chippo," Angelina said, watching him suspiciously.

It was Chippo who took them away, he remembered. It was Chippo who drove them to the road that day in the wagon. You're saying that it was Chippo who sent him back here? Brought him back here? But why? Why? "Chippo?" he said. "Chippo Simon?"

"You know any other Chippo?" Angelina asked. "Phillip, what's wrong with you?"

"Chippo?" he whispered to himself. He looked at her, his face intense, trembling. He leaned closer to her. "When?"

"A month ago."

"A month ago? He saw her a month ago?"

"That's what I hear," Angelina said. "What you so all wound up about? You ain't seen her in years, or even tried to see her."

"How can I get in touch with Chippo? Where is Chippo?"

"How do I know? I don't keep Chippo in my pocket."

"But you said—"

"I didn't say he told it to me. Louis and them heard it in Baton Rouge."

"From who? From Chippo?"

"What you so interested in Chippo for all of a sudden?

What's the matter with you, Phillip? You act like you going crazy."

"I have to see Chippo," he said. "How can I get in touch with Chippo?"

"Lo-re-ta, go to that back door and call Louis in here," Angelina said. "That's 'nough wood."

Loretta Williams groaned as she stood up and walked heavily across the floor back into the kitchen. Phillip swung his chair around and watched her open the back door and speak to the men in the yard. He could hardly wait for them to come inside. Loretta was in front again, walking as slowly and heavily as before. Louis followed her, and two younger men, Jack and Coon, came up single file behind him. All three carried an armload of wood. After laying the wood in the corner, they came to the front of the fireplace. Phillip had already stood up. Before shaking hands with him, Louis rubbed his hand hard across his pant leg. The other two younger men, Jack and Coon, did the same. The three of them were dressed in everyday work clothes—khakis and denims—and they couldn't understand why Phillip, wearing a suit as usual, wanted to shake their hands. They were not church-goers, they didn't follow his civil rights program, and he had never been so friendly toward them before. After shaking hands, Jack and Coon moved back from the fireplace. They were not comfortable around Phillip Martin.

"Nanane told me you saw Chippo Simon," Phillip said to Louis.

"In Baton Rouge last week," Louis said.

"And he had seen Johanna—a lady I used to know—out there in California?"

"Yes sir, that what he said."

"Did he see any of my children?"

"I didn't hear him say nothing 'bout children," Louis said.

"You saw him at his house?"

"A liquor store on East Boulevard."

"You sure it was Chippo?"

"Yes sir; Chippo; that one eye," Louis said, touching under his own eye.

"Chippo," Phillip said thoughtfully. "Chippo. I had just been thinking about Chippo. Listening to y'all chopping wood out there, I was sitting here thinking about how me and Chippo used to chop wood like that. Yeah—Chippo. Chippo Simon. Wouldn't it be Chippo? Of all people—Chippo."

"There he go again," Angelina said. " 'Chippo. Chippo Simon. Wouldn't it be Chippo? Of all people Chippo.' Wouldn't it be Chippo for what, Phillip? Phillip, what's wrong with you? Minute ago you couldn't talk; now you like a parrot and can't stop saying Chippo."

"The sun is breaking through the clouds," Phillip said, still looking at Louis.

"What?" Angelina said.

"Louis, wasn't that sun coming out out there?"

"Well, er, to be factual, Rev, er—"

"Look at me, Louis." Angelina said. "You see any sun coming out out there? Now, 'fore you start lying, know who you lying to."

"Well, er, to be factual, Miss Angy, I, er—"

"Give me a shot out of that bottle, Louis," Phillip said.

"Bottle, Rev?"

"The one in your back pocket."

"Now, Rev—" Louis laughed. "You know I quit drinking."

"What were you doing in that liquor store?" Phillip asked. "What's that on your breath now—frost?"

"Coon?" Louis said, not taking his eye off Phillip.

Coon took the bottle out of his own back pocket and unscrewed the cap and wiped off the mouth of the bottle on his khaki shirtsleeve. The left shirtsleeve was filthy, so he used the right one, which was just as dirty. Finally, he wiped off the bottle with the heel of his thumb, which wasn't too much better, and passed it to Phillip. Phillip turned it up without hesitating.

"Phillip, you done gone plumb crazy?" Angelina screamed at him.

"I used to be able to take it just like you see me there," Phillip told Louis.

"Yes sir," Louis said.

"You much younger than me, Louis, but I'm sure you heard how I used to take it. Me and Chippo. And I used to beat Chippo too."

"Now, wait a minute there, Rev," Louis said. Louis was becoming more and more familiar with Phillip now that Phillip was drinking out of his bottle. "I done heard that Chippo could really put it away. Matter of fact, they say he used to beat Red James, and Red James could—"

"I know what they say, I know what they say, Louis," Phillip said, waving the bottle. "But I used to beat him. Wine, whiskey, gin—name it, and I'd beat him every time."

He turned up the bottle again. "Me and Chippo," he said, after bringing the bottle down. "It had to be Chippo. All them days we used to drink together, play ball together, roam together. Used to go courting together—everything. Then I joined the church, and he just kept on going on his own way. But we brothers still. Soul brothers—that's what you call it, don't you?"

"Yes sir."

"That was me and Chippo—soul brothers. So it had to be Chippo. Chippo."

"Phillip, you losing your mind?" Angelina asked him. "You hear me talking to you, Phillip?"

He took another quick drink from the bottle and passed it back to Coon. Now he turned and looked down at his godmother and started laughing. Everybody was watching him. Louis was proud that Phillip had drunk from his bottle, and he laughed with him. Phillip moved quickly toward his godmother and jerked her chair up off the floor. Angelina screamed and held onto the arms of the rocker. Loretta jumped up and stood back against the wall. The men laughed, and Louis told Angelina to hold tight. Phillip spun around with her two or three times, then set the chair back on the floor. The men were still laughing, but Loretta pressed herself closer to the wall. Angelina, who had caught her breath by now, was looking up at Phillip.

"Kneel down here, Phillip," she said to him.

He was slightly drunk, and also a little dizzy from spinning round the room. He stood back blinking at her a moment, before kneeling by the chair and laying his head in her lap.

"What's the matter, Phillip?" she said, rubbing the side of his face. "Tell Nanane what's the matter."

"Just happy," he whispered. "Happy to hear Chippo's back."

8

Later that evening Phillip drove back to St. Adrienne still thinking about Chippo. Tomorrow he would go into Baton Rouge to find him, and Chippo would explain everything to him. When he came into town he stopped at the St. Adrienne bake shop and ordered a chocolate cake. Tony, the little Italian baker, had heard about his fall and commented on how fast he had recovered. Phillip told him that a little sun was peeping through the clouds. Tony had been outside to dump a garbage can only a few minutes before, and the sky had looked as black as ever. Maybe the minister had some hidden meaning in the words sun and cloud. After taking his money for the cake the baker told Phillip that he wished him the best of luck with Old Chenal on Friday. He said Chenal was a disgrace, and all the good white people of St. Adrienne were ashamed of him. Phillip wanted to say, "To hell with Chenal. My mind is on something more important than all your Chenals." He nodded, gratefully, to the baker, then took the little chocolate cake out to the car and drove home.

When he turned off Choctaw Drive onto St. Anne Street, he noticed the car of his assistant pastor, Jonathan Robillard, parked before his house. Alma was standing on the porch when he drove into the yard. She held the screen door open for him as he came up the steps. He could see that she was worried, and that she had been crying.

"Something the matter?" he asked her.

"Mr. Howard and them inside, waiting to see you."

"See me about what?"

"What do you think, Phillip?"

"I don't know."

"Don't you, Phillip?"

He gave her the box with the cake and went by her into the house. Five members of the St. Adrienne Civil Rights Committee were waiting for him when he came in. Tall, gray-headed Howard Mills sat on the couch with his hat on his knee. Mack Henderson, a small baldheaded man, sat beside Mills. Peter Hebert, who had been trimming his fingernails with a small pearl-handled knife, was the third man on the couch. Sitting in a chair next to him was the secretary of the committee, a light-skinned, heavy-set man called Aaron Brown. Jonathan Robillard was the only one in the room not sitting. He had been pacing the floor the past half hour, and now he stood away from all the others near the piano. Everyone looked at Phillip when he came into the room, but no one said anything until after he spoke.

"Gentlemen."

"Reverend."

Everyone except Jonathan spoke to Phillip. Jonathan was angry.

"Something the matter?" Phillip asked.

"Seems like Chenal up there having himself a little party," Mills said.

"A party?" Phillip said, taking off his hat and overcoat and handing them to Alma, who had followed him inside. Alma took the things from him, but she didn't leave the room.

" 'Varice daughter say he's up there handing out cigars to men, cup cakes to the ladies," Mills said. "Even gived them a hour off to celebrate. 'Varice daughter telephoned my house while all the celebrating was going on."

"Celebrating?" Phillip asked.

"Celebrating," Mills said, nodding his gray head. "And from what I hear your name's on everybody's lip. Seems like you got a lot of white folks up there all a sudden. Counting Chenal."

Phillip looked at all the men on the couch. All except little baldheaded Mack Henderson looked back at him. Mack Henderson kept his head bowed, holding his hat with both hands between his knees. Phillip turned to Jonathan, who was standing by the piano. Jonathan looked at him with disgust.

"I heard you preached well Sunday," Phillip said to him.

"I did the best I could with the short notice I had."

But it was obvious to Phillip that Jonathan didn't want to talk about preaching now.

"Sometimes short notices is all you have," Phillip said. "You have to make the best of it."

It was obvious that Jonathan didn't want to hear any philosophy either.

Phillip turned to Alma.

"Where're the children?"

"In the back."

"Keep them back there. Elijah's here?"

"He was. He left."

"He went up to the Congo Room to get drunk," Jonathan said, behind Phillip. "He was too ashamed to face you."

Phillip didn't look round at him. "Keep the children in the back," he told Alma.

Alma left, and the men in the front could hear her knocking on a door down the hall and talking to the children. Everyone except Mack Henderson was still watching Phillip, who was trying to think how and where to begin.

Phillip unloosened his necktie, then took it off completely and laid it on top of the piano. He turned back to the men sitting on the couch. They were still waiting. Alma had returned to the room. Phillip looked only at her for a moment.

"I wanted you to be the first one to know," he said. "But I see now you have to hear it with the rest. He wouldn't take money. I offered him any reasonable amount. But he wouldn't take it."

"Who wouldn't take money?" Mills asked. "What you talking about?"

"Nolan. Who else?"

"What Nolan got to do with this?"

"Didn't 'Varice daughter tell you?"

"No. She said Chenal was celebrating," Mills said. "Didn't say nothing 'bout Nolan celebrating too. We talking 'bout Chenal. The deal you made with Chenal."

"You know me better than that, Mills," Phillip said. "You think I'd go to Chenal for anything else but to break him?"

"Well, what's he up there celebrating for?" Mills asked. "What they smoking cigars and eating cup cakes for? Mack?"

Little Mack Henderson sitting next to Mills nodded his bald head, but he didn't look at anyone.

"It was between me and Nolan," Phillip said. "Me and Nolan. I went up there to get the boy. Nolan wouldn't take money."

"You still ain't making sense, Phillip," Mills said. "That boy, what he got to do with all this?"

"You mean you still don't know, Mills?" Phillip asked him.

"No," Mills said. "I don't know."

But Phillip could see him thinking.

"Wait," Mills said. "Wait."

Phillip nodded his head.

"Boot," Mills said. "Boot Rey. Mack?"

Mack Henderson looked at Mills. But even after Mills

had called his name, Mills would look at no one else but Phillip. Then suddenly he started nodding his head.

"That's who I seen in that face Saturday. That's who I seen. I knowed it, I knowed it, I knowed I had seen that face somewhere before. It been bothering me ever since. Sunday in church it bothered me. Bothered me last night in bed. Boot Rey. Lucille brother. This boy here grandmother's brother. You remember Boot, don't you, Mack? Boot?"

Mack Henderson nodded his head. "Went North back there in the thirties," he said quietly.

"Had to go," Mills said, still looking at Phillip. "Got in that trouble with them Cajuns on the river and had to go. Had to go fast."

"Yes," Phillip said. "Boot Rey's grandnephew—my son. That's how come I fell. I wasn't tired. I'm not tired now. I recognized my boy cross the room last Saturday. When I started toward him, my legs—my legs just give out from under me."

Alma, who had been listening to all of this as if she couldn't believe what she was hearing, covered her face with her hands and left the room crying. But only Phillip noticed her leaving. The rest of the men looked at him as if they couldn't believe what they had heard either. Mack Henderson, a painfully shy little man, shook his bald head and looked down at the floor. Jonathan, standing by the piano and slightly behind Phillip, looked at him with increasing disgust.

No one said anything for a while, then finally Mills, who had never taken his eyes off Phillip, took in a deep breath and exhaled noisily through his mouth.

"Why you waiting so long to say this, Phillip?" he asked him.

"I wanted to tell somebody, Mills," Phillip said, his voice nearly cracking. "I wanted to say it Saturday. I wanted to say it Sunday when you came in the room. I had a feeling that's what you had on your mind."

"Yes," Mills said. "I hadn't made the connection yet,

but I knowed I knowed that bone. That's what I wanted to talk to you about, but I couldn't think of it in that room for nothing. Thought about it in church, thought about it when I got home. But I hadn't made the connection, and I didn't think I ought to bother you."

"I knowed that was it," Phillip said. "I just had that feeling."

Mills looked across the room at him, his face showing no sympathy at all.

"That's been four days," he said. "Four days you kept this a secret. Telling nobody—not even your wife."

"I wanted to tell her, Mills," Phillip said. "I wanted to tell everybody. I tried to get up. Jonathan is my witness, I tried to get up. More than once I tried to get up."

"The people was still here after you got up," Mills said. "How come you didn't tell them then? Instead of letting Octave tell them that lie?"

"I don't know why I let him do it, Mills," Phillip said. "I don't know why. I been asking myself that same question ever since."

Peter Hebert and Aaron Brown looked across the room at the minister and lowered their eyes. Mack Henderson wouldn't look at him any more. He was fumbling with his hat between his knees. Jonathan standing behind Phillip didn't look at him any more either, but he made it obvious to the others how disgusted he was.

"That was the last time I saw the boy till today," Phillip said to Mills. "I been standing at that window day and night, hoping he would pass by the house again."

"If you wanted to see him so bad, how come you didn't go up there?" Mills asked. "Virginia ain't no more than—what?—seven, eight blocks from here?"

"I know."

"Well, what stopped you?"

"I don't know, Mills. I reckon the same thing that kept me from getting off that floor."

Mills looked at him without sympathy, but as though he had much on his mind.

"So when you heard he was arrested, you went to Nolan?" he asked.

"Yes," Phillip said. "Shepherd came by last night and told me, and I went up there this morning to bail him out. But Nolan wouldn't take money. I told him—I told him I couldn't do it. I told him this was just between me and him, not the people. But he wouldn't hear it. If I wanted my boy —I wanted my boy, Mills. I wanted him bad. I didn't know no other way to get him."

"We have McVay there," Mills said. "These the kind of things he suppose to handle."

"It was personal, Mills. Not political."

"Not political?" Jonathan said, behind Phillip's back. "Not political? Soon as you involved Chenal it was political."

Phillip wouldn't look round at Jonathan. "He's my son, Mills," he said. "I wanted my son."

"We all have sons," Mills said. "Every last one of us in here have sons except Jonathan there. Peter got a son in that same jail right now. I'm sure Nolan would let him out this minute, this minute, if all us went up there and told him we wouldn't demonstrate here no more."

"I couldn't do that," Peter Hebert said, looking cross the room at Phillip. "Not long as we got one Chenal left. No one man got a right to do that."

"I wanted my son, Peter," Phillip said.

"I want mine too," Peter Hebert said. "I want mine out of that jail right now. But I know I don't have no right to ask the people to sacrifice everything for him. No one person can come before the cause, Reverend. Not even you."

"I agree there a hundred percent," Jonathan said, behind Phillip's back.

"The question is what we do about Chenal now?" Aaron Brown asked from his chair.

"We can't do nothing now," Phillip said. "We'll have to wait for another chance."

"You mean you can't do nothing," Jonathan said.

"You neither, boy," Phillip said, without looking round at him. He was getting more and more irritated with Jonathan.

"You're not speaking for me any more," Jonathan said.

Phillip looked back over his shoulder at him this time. "No?" he said.

"No," Jonathan said.

"Then go up there," Phillip said. "Go on up there. He'll pack that jail and throw away the key."

"Because of your mistakes?" Jonathan said. "Your deals? Now everybody must suffer—is that it? Just stop everything we've been working toward, just stop—is that it? Well, not this boy."

Phillip tried to stare him down, but Jonathan wouldn't avert his eyes. Phillip turned back to the others.

"Yes, I made a mistake," he said. "Yes, I shoulda got up off that floor and said who he was. When I didn't do that I shoulda called Mills Saturday night. I shoulda told him about it Sunday morning. Maybe I shoulda called McVay this morning too. These the things I shoulda done—yes, these things I shoulda done. But let's not forget the things I have done in this town, in this parish."

"We've all been out there," Jonathan said, behind his back. "We've all walked the picket line."

"You haven't walked, boy," Phillip said, over his shoulder. "You don't know what walk is."

"I've been out there ever since it started," Jonathan said. "I've been out there since I was fourteen, I'm twenty-two now. I've been kicked, beaten. I've got the scars."

"Trouble with you, you think everything started with the sixties," Phillip said, turning on him. "You don't think there was even a world before the sixties."

"There wasn't any kind of civil rights organization in this town before sixty—sixty-two," Jonathan said. "I know that for a fact, because I was at the first meeting."

"And do you know for a fact, boy, who started the first civil rights organization?"

"You did, Reverend," Jonathan said. "You did. But you couldn't do it by yourself. Without the people behind you, them white people out there wouldn'ta heard a thing you were saying. I'm speaking for the people, Reverend. Something you didn't consider this morning."

"You speaking for one person—Jonathan Robillard," Phillip said. "You envious, you ambitious. You been from the start."

"I'm speaking for the people," Jonathan said. "I'm speaking as a member of this committee. Anybody in the committee feel I'm wrong, let him say so."

"He speaks for me," Peter Hebert said, from the couch.

Phillip jerked round to face the others. Howard Mills was nodding his gray head.

"He speaks for us, Phillip," Mills said.

"I'm president of this committee," Phillip said, thumping his chest. "Me. Not Jonathan. Me."

"You might be president, Phillip," Mills said. "But they got seven of us. Any time four of us decide on any one thing, that's the way the thing go. The president vote's just one vote. Even you 'greed to that."

"What you trying to say to me, Mills?" Phillip asked. "You trying to say y'all done elected Jonathan behind my back? Jonathan is the great spokesman now?"

"Nobody ain't elected nobody, Phillip," Mills said, getting to his feet. "But we been talking—no point trying to hide that." He dropped his hat on the couch where he had been sitting, then he turned back to Phillip. "I know how you must feel," he said. "I know how you musta felt this morning with Nolan. I have sons too. One I ain't seen nearly long as you hadn't seen that boy. I hear from him, he send me little money now and then, but he won't come home. That's what we working for, Phillip, so our boys will come back home. So they won't have to leave from home. That's why people like Chenal have to go."

"You think I didn't think about that this morning?" Phillip asked.

"Maybe you did, maybe you didn't."

"Maybe, Mills? Maybe?"

"I wasn't there, Phillip. None of us was there. Just you and Nolan."

"You want to call Nolan on that telephone?"

Mills stood back, very straight and tall, and looked him fully in the face.

"I'm not interested in Nolan, Phillip. I'm interested in that old peckerwood up there called Albert Chenal. That's the only person I'm interested in."

"Chenal is just another battle. Not the war, Mills."

"He was my war," Mills said. "I'm old, I don't have too many more battles left in me. This might be my last one—and I wanted to go out winning. I wanted Chenal. Because I know Chenal. I've knowed Chenal long as I've knowed you, Phillip. I knowed his daddy. They didn't have that big store then—a smaller one little farther up the river. Thomas Chenal—I knowed him. I worked for him. I know what he was. I know how he felt about black women. No black woman looking any way presentable couldn't come in his store if he didn't go after her. I remember when he raped Elliot Toussaint daughter. I was working for him—I remember the day. Winter, just like now. He raped her, and she run out the store crying. He grabbed up one of them old cheap pocketbooks and stuffed a pair stockings in it and throwed it out after her. Told the people she had enticed him, and that's what he had paid her with. That she dropped it out there on the sidewalk when she left. But I knowed he raped her. I knowed it then. I was just too scared to say a word."

Mills walked around the room as he spoke. He wasn't talking only to Phillip, but to the rest of the men as well. They were all listening, but, except for Jonathan, they wouldn't look at him. They felt that he was talking about their cowardice as well as his own.

"That wasn't the only one," Mills said, from the door. He had just pulled the curtains aside to look out on the street. But now he was facing the men again. "That wasn't the only one he raped one way or another. That mulatto schoolteacher, Christophe, that's his boy. No more Christophe than I'm a Christophe. Just go by Joe Christophe's name because he can't go by Chenal. That's Tom Chenal boy—Albert Chenal brother. They had more—many more. It was depression. Sometime the woman was the only one putting bread on that table. I done seen it, I done seen it. This time a dress for your little girl; next time pants for your little boy. Next time fifty cents—six bits—a dollar. I done seen it. I hated it, but I was too coward. I told myself was nothing I could do. That's how you live with yourself; you tell yourself ain't nothing you can do."

He stopped again and looked at Phillip. But neither Phillip, nor any of the others, except for Jonathan, would look back at him. Jonathan felt that Mills was talking only about the older men in the room.

"You told Jonathan they had a world out there 'fore the sixties," Mills went on. "You right, they had a world out there. But 'fore the sixties people round here wasn't doing nothing to change that world. Sixty I was already an old man—in my seventies—I'm eighty-four now. But not till then, till the sixties, I found a way to go 'gainst Chenal, and the likes of Chenal. Tom was dead, but his son car' his seeds, and he ain't no better. He's got no more respect for me, for you, for any other black man or woman than his paw had. We animals far as he's concerned. Baboons, monkeys, apes. Me? He call me an old gray coon. Don't think I'm even good enough for the ape family."

Mills laughed to himself. Peter Hebert and Aaron Brown laughed too. Aaron was very light-skinned, and his face turned quite red when he laughed. Jonathan didn't see any humor in it at all.

"No, Chenal ain't just another battle, Phillip," Mills was saying. "It's war. Plain, cold war. 'Look, Chenal, we ain't baboons and apes—I'm sure no old gray coon. We men, Chenal, and we 'tend to fight you till we change you or destroy you. We got nothing but our bodies to use for weapons, but we go'n use that till we get what we want. Respect for our women, our children, respect for the dead who couldn't get respect from your paw.' "

Mills stopped again to look at Phillip. Phillip kept his eyes to the floor. But everyone else was looking at Mills now. Even little Mack Henderson would occasionally raise his head.

"But now I hear from my leader I can't even use that—the only weapon I have—my own body. This got to be the worse thing happen to us since we organized this committee. We been beatened—all us in here. Throwed in that jail—every last one of us. But we held the committee together. We put this little town on the map, 'cause we held together. Newspapers, television, done visited us from all over the state, 'cause we was like a tight fist—holding together. All over the country people been watching—'cause we been holding together. Till today."

He was quiet again, but never taking his eyes off Phillip. Phillip, who had been staring down at the floor all the time, now raised his head to look back at Mills.

"I told you why I did it, Mills," he said calmly. "But it look like I'm the only one in here who woulda done so. We all love our children, want our children, but it look like I'm the only one who woulda done what I did."

"We want this world better fit for everybody children, Phillip," Mills said. "Not just for one man."

"Still, I'm only a man," Phillip said. "Only a man—and a father."

"Every last man in here is a father, except for Jonathan over there," Mills said. "And one day he'll be one too. But till we get rid of people like Chenal, change people like Chenal, Jonathan son'll have to go through the same thing mine did. His son'll have to work for Chenal for nothing—or, worse yet, leave home. We want Jonathan son to stay home, Phillip."

"That's all I wanted too, Mills, my son in my home," Phillip said. "That's all. Nothing else. And I still say Chenal is a battle, not the war. And one day we'll get Chenal. I have that kind of faith in my people."

"But will I be here?" Mills asked.

"I don't know if I'll be here," Phillip told him. "Maybe none of us. Maybe not even Jonathan there. But the people will be. We done put something in the mind of the people, they won't let go that easy."

"The people wasn't thinking about next year, or year after next, Phillip," Mills said. "They been thinking about Friday. With you in front. You, me, Jonathan—the rest. But you in front."

"Ain't I been out front all the time, Mills?"

"All the time, Phillip," Mills agreed, nodding his head. "That's why they expected you out there this time too. Well, what do we say to the people?"

"I did what I had to do, Mills," Phillip said.

"Give them up for the boy?"

"A battle. Not them. A battle, Mills."

"I don't think they go'n know the difference, Phillip," Mills said. "Because I don't know the difference. I don't know if Peter know the difference—with a boy in that jail right now. Peter, you know the difference?" Mills asked.

"No, I don't know the difference," Peter said.

"I don't think anybody else in here know the difference either, Phillip," Mills said.

"I did what I had to do," Phillip said. "I made a mistake, and I'm ready to admit it. But I did what I had to do.

Three times I offered him money—three times. He wouldn't take it. I didn't have no other choice."

"Well, we come up here to do something too," Jonathan said, coming from round the piano and over to where the other men were sitting. "We come up here to listen and make a decision. I've been listening, and now I think we ought to vote like we said we'd do."

"Vote?" Phillip said, looking at Mills, not at Jonathan.

"Yes, Phillip, vote," Mills said.

"Vote on what?" Phillip asked. "I've already said we can't go up there Friday."

"We know that," Mills said. "That's not what we voting on."

"What else can you vote on?" Phillip asked.

"Whether you go'n stay president of this committee, Phillip," Mills said. "Nobody but the president coulda done what you did. He wouldn'ta listened to nobody else. Now we voting to see if you fit to be president, to make them kind of decisions."

Phillip stared at Mills as though he could not believe what he was hearing. He looked round at all the others. All were watching him, except for little Mack Henderson who kept his head bowed. He looked back at Mills again, his jaws set so tight that his face trembled.

"Whether I'm fit to be president," he said. "Whether I'm fit to be president. If I'm not fit to be president, who the hell in this room is?"

"We got a quorum," Mills said. "We can vote on that."

"Behind my back—whether I'm fit," Phillip said, staring at Mills.

"You went behind backs too, Phillip," Mills said, challenging him. "If you had come out in the open and told people who that boy was, none of this never woulda happened. But for four days you knowed, and you wouldn't say a thing to nobody. For four days—and still you wouldn't even go to your own wife. You went behind her back too.

Your children backs. Not just the committee—the church, the community. You made your own decision all by yourself. And, yes, I say we vote to see if you fit to be president. Mack?" Mills said, looking down at Mack Henderson.

Little Mack Henderson shook his bald head. He wouldn't look up. Mills continued to look down at him.

"Well, man, you voting, or you ain't?" Mills asked.

Mack Henderson shook his head again. He had begun to sweat, and a white speck of light shone on his shiny scalp.

"Peter?" Mills said.

"No man ought to have that kind of authority," Peter said. But he wouldn't look at Phillip when he spoke.

"Aaron?" Mills asked.

"I have to agree," Aaron said. "If one man can do it, why not every man, at any time?"

Mills looked at Jonathan. He didn't have to ask him. He knew how he was voting.

"I vote that Reverend Phillip J. Martin be removed as president of the St. Adrienne Civil Rights Committee," Jonathan said.

Mills stared at him. Not for the pompous way he had spoken, but he wanted to remind him that it was he, Jonathan, who had suggested holding a meeting and voting. Mills also wanted him to know that he, Jonathan, would be the next president, and that it would be his responsibility to make all the right moves. Jonathan looked steadily back at Mills. He was ready for the challenge.

"I vote with the majority," Mills said. "Hawkins ain't here, but we got four, that's enough."

"So I'm out as president, is that it?" Phillip asked.

"The committee voted that way," Mills said.

"And Mr. Jonathan, there, he's going to be the new president?"

"The committee hasn't voted yet."

"Sure," Phillip said. "Sure." He looked at Jonathan, who stood beside Mills looking very confident in himself. He had already taken on the pose of a new president, he was already feeling self-important. "So it's up to you now, huh, boy?" Phillip said to him. "You fit to pass the word on to the people, huh? Not just the black and the white, but the Chenals and the Nolans—you the one most fit, huh?" Phillip grinned at him. "Boy, you got no idea what you up against. You think you know. Just 'cause you been out there eight years, you think you know, huh? You don't know your ass from a hole in the ground. You don't know your right hand from your left."

"I'll learn," Jonathan said.

"You'll learn?" Phillip asked him. "You think they go'n give you time to learn out there? They ain't go'n even give you time to think. You think that's a Sunday school out there, you think that's what it is? Wait till you go up against somebody like Nolan."

"I'm not afraid of Nolan," Jonathan said with confidence.

"I know that," Phillip said. "You don't have enough sense to be scared of him—and that's the danger, you not scared of nobody. But you go'n find out bravery ain't all. Knowing when to move and what to say is just as important. And, boy, you got a lot to learn. Not just about white people, which takes more than any eight years; you got a lot to learn about your own people. You don't even know nothing about them yet."

"I'll learn fast," Jonathan said. "And I won't forget who I'm working with, and who I'm working for."

"Sure, boy," Phillip said. "Sure. Now get the hell out of my house before I throw you out."

"I don't think you need to talk like that, Phillip," Mills said.

"No?" Phillip said.

"No," Mills said.

"That's all right, Brother Mills," Jonathan said. "I'm on my way." He went as far as the door and turned to look back at Phillip. "I'm go'n break Chenal," he said. "We can't go against him Friday because you've fixed it that way. But I'm go'n break him."

"You'll break that Chenal, boy, I have no doubt of that," Phillip said. "But you go'n always have a Chenal. I have no doubt that one day you'll even be a Chenal."

Jonathan grinned at him and turned to the others. "Gentlemen, I'll be waiting outside."

Aaron Brown and Peter Hebert followed Jonathan out of the room. Little Mack Henderson started toward the door, but stopped and looked back at Phillip. More than once he attempted to say something, but finally gave up and left the room shaking his head.

"I'm sorry this happened, Phillip," Mills said. "Everybody out there is sorry this had to happen. But what else could we do, just forget it?"

"We all did what we thought was right," Phillip said.

Mills picked up his hat from the couch.

"Why is that boy here, Phillip?" he asked.

"He came here to kill me, Mills. Kill me for raping his mother—almost thirty years ago."

"That's crazy," Mills said. "You didn't rape nobody."

Phillip looked at him. "Didn't I, Mills?"

"You loved her," Mills said. "She loved you. I can remember that."

"That's right, we loved each other," Phillip said, nodding his head. "We loved each other. But right now, Mills, I can't even 'call that boy's name. Tell them that for me, Mills. Tell them why I got my son out of jail. I just wanted to know his name."

He left the room. But Mills didn't move. He felt very bad. He felt very tired. He walked out the front door, wondering if he and the others had done the right thing.

Phillip went back into the kitchen and got one of the bottles of sherry and a glass and went to his office. The bottle had not been opened, and he ripped off the seal and half filled the glass. He drank it quickly, and he could feel it sweet and warm going down into the pit of his stomach. He poured more into the glass, this time nearly filling it. Then he stopped up the bottle and sat in the chair behind his desk. It was dark in the room, but he wouldn't draw back the curtains or turn on the lights. He didn't want to see himself thinking. He didn't want to think at all, especially about what had happened only a few minutes ago, because he didn't want to get mad. Still, he couldn't help but think. And the more he thought the angrier he became. And the angrier he became, the more he drank. When he took a good look at the bottle he saw that he had drunk more than half of it, and he pushed it across the desk away from him.

I don't know what the hell is going on, he thought. This must be a dream. This got to be a dream. Everything since last Saturday's been one long nightmare. What the hell is going on, I don't know.

How can I stand in my own house and let them bastards tell me I'm not fit to run this thing? I'm not fit. After all the work I've done. After I break the ground, after I show them how to plant the corn, then I'm not fit. I'm not fit. I shoulda knocked the hell out of Jonathan and throwed him and his little fit ass out of my house.

This got to be a dream, Phillip told himself again. I ain't woke up from that fall yet. I'm still down there on the floor. I didn't go to Nolan, I didn't talk to that boy, I didn't visit Nanane. And surely I didn't stand in my own house and listen to that crap. No, I must still be on that floor.

But he knew he wasn't on the floor and he wasn't still asleep. He drank the last of the wine in the glass and pushed the glass away. Now he stared at the glass and the bottle. When was the last time he had done anything like this? He had never drunk in front of his godmother before, and he couldn't remember the last time he had drunk alone.

He looked toward the door that led out into the hall. The house was quiet. He had not heard a word out of the children since coming home, and nothing from Alma either, since she went into the bedroom. He had to go to her—but say what to her. And say what to the children?

He looked at the bottle and the glass, but he changed his mind about drinking any more. He stood up, feeling very tired and a little drunk, and he steadied himself by holding on to the end of the desk. Then he left the office and went across the hall into the bedroom. Alma lay on top the covers, facing the wall.

"You go'n catch cold," he told her.

She didn't answer him.

"It's getting late," he said. "Don't you think you ought to start supper?"

She still didn't answer him, and he went around the other side of the bed to face her.

"I'm sorry," he said.

"Sorry about what, Phillip?" she said without looking at him.

"Everything," he said.

"It's all right."

"It's not all right," he said. "I shoulda come to you."

"I'm not that important, Phillip."

"You are," he said.

"I'm not. I always knowed that."

"That's not true, Alma."

She didn't answer. She faced the wall, the left side of her face down in the covers. The spread was wet from where she had been crying.

He sat down on the bed beside her.

"I didn't come to you because I didn't know how to come to you. I didn't know if you'd understand."

"That's how it's always been," she said. "You come to me for this bed, for nothing else."

"That's not true."

She looked up at him now. "That is true, Phillip. For this bed. Cook your food. Follow you to that church. That's all you married me for. You never come to me for any kind of problem. Now you try to do the same thing to them. But they won't take it."

"I pity little men."

"That's right—little men, Phillip," Alma said. "That's why they did what they did. They know you look at them as little men."

"I made one mistake. How about all the other things I've done?"

"This was big for them. Especially Mr. Howard."

"Getting my boy out that jail was big for me, too," he said. "But nobody else can see that. Not even you."

He was tired, and he shut his eyes and covered his face with both hands.

"I have to go to Baton Rouge," he said, looking at her again. "I have to see Chippo Simon. I heard that Chippo seen the boy out there in California, and I have to talk to him."

Alma was facing the wall again.

"You listening to me?" he asked her.

"Go on to Baton Rouge if you have to go to Baton Rouge, Phillip," she said.

"I want you to talk to the children for me."

She looked at him again. "Me talk to the children?" she asked. "Say what to the children, Phillip? Say something about their brother? Say what about their brother? I didn't talk to their brother, you did. Look like you ought to be the one talking to the children."

"I don't know how," he said.

"After all that's happened, you still don't know how?" she asked him. "Well, I don't know how, neither." And she faced the wall again.

Phillip got up from the bed. "I have to go to Baton Rouge," he said. "I have to go find Chippo."

He went around the bed to get his hat and overcoat from the closet.

"Why don't you get up from there before you catch cold," he said, looking at her. "Or get under the cover."

She didn't answer him, and he came around the bed to face her again.

"Alma, what you want me to say? What you want me to say I ain't said already?"

"Nothing," she said.

He sat down beside her and put his hand on her shoulder.

"I'll make it up to you when I come back," he said.

"Don't worry about making up to me, Phillip. Just make up to your children."

"What you talking like that for?"

"You never worried about making up to me before."

"I never told you all my problems because I didn't want you worrying every time I left the house."

"That's not it," she said. She turned over on her back and looked up at him. Her eyes were red from crying, and he could see the imprint of the spread against the side of her face. "That's not why you never included me," she said. "You never included me because you wanted to do it all yourself. Ever since I met you, Phillip, you been running, running, and running. Away from what, Phillip? Trying to make up for what, Phillip? For what you did to that boy? For what you did to his mon? For other things you did in the past? The past is the past, Phillip. You can't make up for the past. There ain't nothing you go'n find out in Baton Rouge. Nothing Mr. Chippo can tell you."

"I have to go anyhow."

"Sure, you have to go," Alma said. "You always do what you want. This morning you did what you wanted. That's why they voted you out. They can't let you treat them like you treat me."

"You ready to vote me out too?"

"That's up to you, Phillip."

"What d'you mean?"

"That's if you still want me here?"

"I ever said anything else?"

"Not with words—no. By your action, many times."

"You never said it before."

"I been saying it for years, Phillip. You never had time to hear me."

He stood up.

"I have to go," he said.

"You ain't go'n find out nothing in Baton Rouge, Phillip. Not a thing."

He put on the overcoat and hat.

"What brought my boy back here, or what sent him back here I'll find out in Baton Rouge. That's important to me. I want to reach my boy. What I did this morning it seems like it's wrong to lot of people, but if he was in that jail right now, and that was all I had to offer, I'd do it all over again. I've paid some dues in this town, some heavy dues. Your life's been threatened, my children's lives been threatened, mine been threatened. All because I kept pushing for the people out there. Crosses burnt on my lawn, my house been shot in, my church been shot up—all because I kept pushing for the people out there. Well, this morning I pushed a little bit for myself, and I don't care what the people think."

"And me? You care what I think, Phillip?"

"Long as you don't say stay away from Baton Rouge—'cause I'm going to Baton Rouge. When I come back I'll make it up to you, if I have to start from scratch."

"There ain't nothing in Baton Rouge, Phillip."

"I'll have to find that out for myself."

He went out the room. A moment later Patrick came in. He sat on the bed beside his mother and passed his hand over the side of her face. But she was still thinking about Phillip, and she seemed oblivious to the boy being there.

Even when she took his small hand and held it to her lips, it was done more from instinct than awareness of him in particular. When she finally looked at him she wondered what she would do if someone tried to take him away from here. She took his face in her hands and began kissing him. Then she held him close to her body while looking toward the door.

9

When Phillip crossed the Mississippi River Bridge into Baton Rouge he went into the first gas station he saw. He had not come in to buy gas—the tank was more than half full—he had come in to check his address book. He knew that most of the people in the book knew Chippo Simon, but he didn't know which of these would know where Chippo lived. Besides that, he didn't want to go to someone's house who would ask him a lot of questions and keep him talking the rest of the evening. He wanted to find Chippo soon as possible and go back home.

Phillip heard someone tapping on the window, and he looked out at a black youth wearing a wool cap with muffs pulled down over his ears. The boy stood in the bright lights of the gas station, his hot breath steaming the outside of the window. Phillip shook his head. The boy didn't understand, and Phillip rolled down the glass.

"Just checking my book," he said, showing the little black address book to the boy.

"You go'n have to pull up," the boy said.

"Would you happen to know Mr. Chippo Simon?" Phillip asked him.

"Who?" the boy said, checking Phillip closely. He was suspicious of strangers who wore clothes as expensive as Phillip's.

"Mr. Chippo Simon," Phillip repeated. "About my age. I'm probably little bigger." He touched under his right eye. "One bad eye," he said.

"I know Chippo," the boy said, still looking closely at Phillip.

"You know where he lives?" Phillip asked.

"Round East Boulevard, I reckon," the boy said. "That's where I'm always seeing him."

"You don't know what street?"

"No," the boy said. "That's all you want?"

"Yes. Thank you kindly," Phillip said.

"You can check on East Boulevard," the boy said. "Somebody there might can help you."

"Thank you," Phillip said.

To East Boulevard from the gas station was only three or four blocks. At one time East Boulevard was the center of business and entertainment for blacks in Baton Rouge. Phillip could remember when Chippo and he used to come here to gamble and dance. Everything they had wanted, from a woman to a good barroom fight, could be found on East Boulevard or nearby. It was a dangerous place, you could easily get yourself killed there, but he was much younger then, and he didn't mind taking chances.

But the place had changed. Twenty years ago it was lively, now it was dead. Many of the bars, cafés, and other small businesses had shut down. The remaining buildings looked old and dilapidated. The street had never been lighted well, but it looked even darker now. The sidewalks were paved in some places, dirt and gravel in others. The people walked in the street to escape the mud and puddles of water from all the rain the past few days.

Phillip looked out at the people he met, but he didn't recognize anyone. After going a half dozen blocks he turned around and started back. Now he looked at the people he had passed before and still didn't see anyone he knew. He tried to think of someone to call, someone who would give him the information he needed and not talk the rest of the night. He remembered a woman on Tennessee Street that Chippo used to live with—but, no, he wouldn't call Lelia. He couldn't think of anybody else in the world who talked more than she did. He tried to recall if Louis had told him where on East Boulevard he had seen Chippo. But why would Chippo be there again? If Chippo was anything like he used to be he never stayed in any one place or with any one woman too long. Phillip went up to North Boulevard and turned around again.

He saw a man in a black overcoat walking on the sidewalk to his right. The man had both hands in his pockets, his head down, his shoulders hunched, walking fast against the wind. Phillip drove up even with him and rolled down the glass.

"Pardon me—"

The man kept his steady pace without even glancing round. Phillip thought he had not heard him.

"Pardon me," he said, driving alongside him. "Do you know—"

The man stopped quickly and turned on him. Phillip could see in his face that he was angry.

"You got a problem?" the man asked.

"I was go'n ask if you know Chippo Simon?" Phillip said.

"Do I look like any goddamn phone book?"

"I'm sorry I bothered you," Phillip said.

He had leaned all the way over to the other door, now he moved back under the wheel.

"Chippo live somewhere up round yonder," the man said, jerking his head up the street and to the left. "I don't know what house he live in, what street, and I don't care. That's good enough for you?"

Phillip nodded and drove off. After going a little distance, he looked through the rear-view mirror at the man walking again.

"Wouldn't like to be his wife when he get home," he said to himself.

He thought about Alma and the children in St. Adrienne, and he knew he had to hurry and find Chippo and go back to them. He turned left off East Boulevard onto Louise Street. The car lights flashed on someone walking in the street up ahead of him. When he got closer he saw there were two women walking in single file. Phillip started to go by them without saying anything, but changed his mind and stopped. Both women wore overcoats, both wore scarves on their heads, which also covered their ears to protect them from the cold. Phillip saw that the woman in front, the larger of the two and the lighter-skinned, carried a set of rosaries. The other one, who carried a shopping bag, smiled warmly at Phillip as the two of them stepped up to the car. Phillip told them that he was a good friend of Chippo Simon, and he had been told that Chippo lived somewhere round here, but he didn't know exactly where.

"Geneva, you know where Chippo live?" the woman with the rosaries asked the other.

"Somewhere over there," Geneva said, motioning to the left with the shopping bag. "Pecan, Swart—one of them over there. Always see him walking in that direction."

"You ladies going that way?" Phillip asked them.

"Yes, but it's only a couple more blocks; we can walk."

"I'll be glad to drop you off—that's if your husbands don't mind."

"Well, that's surely no problem there," the woman with the rosaries said.

She opened the door to let the woman with the shopping bag get in first. After they had settled down in the back seat, Phillip drove away.

"Getting colder and colder," the woman with the rosaries said. "Freeze before morning. We just come from the church. Lit some candles for my boy."

"I see," Phillip said.

"Died in a wreck three years ago. On graduation day."

"I'm sorry to hear that," Phillip said.

"Seems like it was no more than yesterday," the woman said. "You from round here? Can't seem to place you."

"Cross the river. St. Adrienne."

"Oh yes—St. Adrienne. Nice little town—St. Adrienne. We have people in St. Adrienne—all along that St. Charles River. Maybe you're acquainted with some—LeBlancs?"

"I know a few LeBlancs," Phillip said. "Gilbert, Octave, Sheree."

"All them's my kin," the woman with the rosaries said. "This is my sister Geneva. My name's Theresa."

"Glad to know you ladies," Phillip said, looking in the rear-view mirror at them. "I'm Phillip Martin."

"Oh yes, the minister from St. Adrienne," Theresa said. "Shoulda recognized you. Have seen you in the papers and on television. That's Reverend Martin," she said to Geneva.

"Now, that's something, isn't it?" Geneva said, and smiled again. "Just can't tell who might give you a ride these days."

"Yes, indeed," Theresa said. "We're always hearing about you. Been doing some good work in St. Adrienne."

Phillip thought about what had happened to him only a couple of hours ago. "Always tried to do my best," he said.

"What more can poor people do?" Theresa said. "Turn left right there."

After he had gone another block she told him to turn right. Phillip turned down a street so narrow that the weeds along the wire fence brushed against the side of the car. Theresa told him to stop at the last driveway on the right just before he came to the cross street.

"I suppose you heard about the killing?" she said.

"Killing?" Phillip said, looking at her in the rear-view mirror.

"They killed one of our people today."

"I haven't heard."

"Happened round four o'clock. He took some food and ran home. The white people who owned the store knew who he was and sent the law after him. The law came, guns drawn, and called him out. But they don't wait for him to come out, they bust in the house and start shooting. Grazed couple of the other children and killed him. A soldier, too. Had been a soldier in the war—Viet Nam. They claimed he was going for a gun when they killed him. Shot him in the back."

"A nice boy," Geneva said quietly.

"My own children growed up with him," Theresa said. "He used to stay there in the house. How many times I've fed him there with my other children. Him and Mathias—like brothers. Mathias was my son who was killed in the wreck three years ago, on his graduation day. Seems like it was just yesterday."

"They will kill ours," Geneva said quietly, as before.

"Yes," Theresa said. "They send our children to war. When they come back they give them nothing to do—no jobs, no nothing. When they steal food to eat they kill them. What a world."

In the rear-view mirror, Phillip could see Geneva touching her sister on the arm to comfort her. Theresa nodded her head and fingered the rosaries.

"Yes," she said. "He sees all. It's all written down."

Phillip stopped at the driveway just before reaching the cross street. A screen door slammed at the house on the right, and a small child ran across the driveway toward the car.

"Just look at that," Theresa said. "I bet you she don't have shoe one on her foot. Go back inside, Keli. Where's her mon? Bet you she's laying cross that bed 'sleep. Where's her paw? Go back inside, Keli."

The child pressed her small brown face against the window and smiled at Phillip. He smiled back at her. He thought about his own children at home that he could not go to.

"Would you like to come inside and have a cup of coffee, Reverend?" Theresa asked.

"No, thank you kindly," Phillip said. "I want to find Chippo and head on back."

"Well, if you change your mind feel free to drop by," she said. "People round here drink coffee all day long and half the night. Till they fall asleep, babies drink it too."

She opened the door to get out, and Phillip could hear the rosaries rattling in her hand. Geneva had already gotten out on the other side.

"Swart's over there," Geneva said, nodding toward the left. "I'm pretty sure it's Swart where he's staying now."

Swart Street was two blocks long and just as narrow as the street Phillip had just left. As on the other street, most of the houses were old, weather-gray, and dark. After going half a block, the lights of the car flashed on a man coming toward Phillip. The man, tall, thin, in a black overcoat and black cowboy hat, was taking those short, hesitant steps that a drunk must take to stay on his feet. Phillip was a little doubtful about asking this one about Chippo Simon, but he didn't see anyone else. The drunk stuck his head inside the window soon as the car stopped, and now Phillip wished he had kept going.

"Do you know if Chippo Simon live down here?" he asked the drunk.

"You looking for Chippo?" the drunk asked him.

Phillip nodded his head, and tried not to draw breath.

The drunk, with his head still in the window, shut one eye very tight, the other one barely opened, and pointed up the street.

"Right there," he said.

He could have been pointing toward any one of a half dozen houses, on either side of the road.

"Which one?" Phillip asked.

The drunk was very tired. He had to rest a while. Then he sighted carefully. "That one."

He was definitely pointing to the houses on the left now, but Phillip still could not tell exactly which one. He was glad the drunk had turned his head.

The drunk rested another second. "See that screen?" he asked.

"Yes."

"That's not it," he said, and shook his head. He rested again. "Next one," he said, when he had enough energy to speak. "Shotgun house."

"Thank you kindly," Phillip said.

The drunk turned his head. He wanted to say, "Oh, that's all right." But when he looked at Phillip he had either forgotten what he had intended to say or he was too tired to say it. He gave a half-hearted wave of his right hand and walked away. Phillip smiled to himself and drove on.

But when he stopped before the house, he saw that the house was dark. Still, he got out of the car to see if Chippo was there. Halfway up the walk he heard a woman's voice from the screen porch of the next house. It was very dark on the porch, and he could hardly see the woman at all through the screen. He wasn't sure she was speaking to him, and he continued on up the walk.

"He ain't there," the woman said again. The voice was as inflectionless as it was the first time.

"I'm looking for Chippo Simon," Phillip said. "This where he lives?"

"Most the time."

Phillip looked again toward the little shotgun house with its one door facing the street. The door was shut tight, and he could tell that there was not a light on inside.

"You have any idea when he'll be back?" Phillip spoke to the woman behind the screen.

The woman didn't answer. It was so dark behind the screen that Phillip couldn't tell whether she was looking at him or not. He turned back toward the car.

"You can wait for him in there if you want," the woman said. "He never latch that door."

"You expect him back soon?"

"You talking 'bout Chippo Simon?" the woman asked.

"Yes," Phillip said.

"How well you know Chippo Simon?"

"We grew up together," Phillip said.

"Then you ought to know better than to ask that kind of question."

Phillip got back into his car.

"If you see him 'fore I do you tell him he better bring me my money on back here," the woman said.

Phillip didn't know whether to stay there and wait for Chippo or go somewhere else and come back later. He thought about the two Catholic women who had invited him in for coffee. They were nice people. Maybe he ought to go by there. But wouldn't they ask questions too? Eventually they would have to ask why he, Phillip Martin, was looking for somebody like Chippo Simon. How could he explain to them what it was all about? How could he explain to any stranger what it was all about? Did Alma understand? Did Mills? Jonathan? How could a total stranger understand?

He thought about the young man who was killed today. He wondered if he knew his people and if he could do anything to help. He looked back over his shoulder, and he could see that the woman was still out on the porch. He got out of the car again.

"Pardon me," he said. "You know the young man who was killed this evening?"

"One of them Turner boys off Maximillian," the woman said.

"Thank you," he said, and got back into the car. He knew Turners in Baton Rouge, but he didn't know any on Maximillian Street. He wondered if they could be related. He looked back over his shoulder at the woman, but changed his mind about asking her any more questions. After sitting there another ten minutes trying to decide what he ought to do with his time, he finally drove away. At the end of the street he glanced at his watch. It was exactly seven o'clock. He was so tired he couldn't believe it wasn't much later. He wondered how long it would be before he found Chippo and went back home.

He drove aimlessly up one street and down another. He passed by a theater where he had gone to movies many years ago. On the marquee was an advertisement of black actors in a gangster film. Life-size posters tacked to the wall showed a black actor shooting two guns simultaneously. Whatever he was shooting at wasn't shown in the picture. Phillip thought about the young man who was killed today and grunted to himself. After going another couple of blocks he passed a bar where he used to drink and gamble. Behind the bar was a roominghouse where he had taken his women. He remembered that on Mondays and Thursdays there were always sheets on the clothesline in the back yard.

He drove uptown to the old State Capitol, which was now used as a museum, then he drove along the railroad tracks until he came to a cross street that took him back to Chippo's house. But he could see there still wasn't any light on inside, and he kept on going. On East Boulevard he stopped in front of a little gray stucco building. Only half of the red-and-green neon sign which gave its name, *Dettie's Dinette*, was in working order. NO BETTER CREOLE FOOD SERVED ANYWHERES ELSE was carelessly painted in large black letters on the wall facing the street. Phillip thought Dettie's Dinette looked safe enough for a cup of coffee and went in.

Two people were in the café. An old man wearing a black overcoat was in one of the booths against the wall. A heavy-set, brown-skinned woman wearing a white dress and a knitted wool sweater sat on a stool behind the counter.

"How is it out there?" she asked.

"It's getting there," he said.

"You can feel it every time you open that door," the woman said.

"A cup of coffee," Phillip said.

The woman groaned as she pushed herself away from the stool. She poured the coffee from a glass urn that sat on a little electrical stove at the far end of the counter.

"This been some weather, you hear me," she said, coming back to Phillip with the coffee.

Phillip paid her and went to a booth against the wall. He sat with his back to the old man; he could see that the woman had taken her seat again.

It was quiet for a while.

"Did you hear about the killing?" the woman said from behind the counter.

"Yes," Phillip said.

"Broke in the house while they was sitting at the table eating. Poor Evelyn. It's over for the boy—but what she must be going through?"

"They any kins to the Turners in Fairfield?" Phillip asked.

"I don't think I know any Turners in Fairfield," the woman said.

"What's her husband's name?" Phillip asked.

"She don't have a husband," the woman said. "Just her and them children. Now the oldest one gone."

In his mind Phillip could see the woman and her children huddled together crying. But there would be other women there too, patting her on the shoulder and telling her: "Take courage, *cher*; take courage; He never give you no more than you can bear." Phillip clenched his fist and held it like that a while.

He started thinking about his own family at home. How

was he ever going to make up to Alma and the children? How was he ever going to make up to his church? But maybe he wouldn't even have a church when he got back. Maybe they had taken that away from him too.

He drank some of the hot coffee and set the cup back down. He was staring at the woman but not seeing her. He was oblivious to everything round him. A moment after he had drunk the coffee he couldn't remember if he had raised the cup to his mouth.

He was still thinking about the ones at home. He was thinking about Mills and the others now. He could understand why they couldn't understand. If someone had told him a month ago—no, a week ago—that he would be sitting here tonight waiting for Chippo to explain something that had happened in his life more than twenty years ago he wouldn't have been able to believe that either.

But why was he here? Why? Why couldn't he just forget it like the rest did? Men see their bastards walking by the house every day—some even joke about it. He had done the same. This was not his only child out of wedlock. He had children that he knew of by three or four other women. And he had been as proud of it as any other man. So why was he here now? Why was he sitting in this cold little café waiting for Chippo? What could Chippo give him? What could Chippo say?

Maybe nothing, he told himself. But maybe he can tell me his name. And that would be more than I know.

The coffee was cold when he raised the cup to his mouth this time. And as he set the cup back down on the table he noticed the woman staring at him. No, not at him, but at someone behind him. He glanced back over his shoulder. The old man from the other booth was standing over him. He was a thin, brown-skinned man who could have been in his seventies or even eighties. The old black overcoat he wore was much too big and hung too far to one side. A Bible of wrinkled brown leather was stuck under his right armpit. The man looked very tired, his eyes watery and bloodshot.

"It's all right," Phillip told the woman.

"I don't mind if he come in here to warm, but I don't want him bothering my customers," the woman said.

"It's no bother," Phillip said. "Can we have another cup of coffee?"

The woman brought the coffee urn and an extra cup to the table. The old man had sat down on the bench opposite Phillip.

"Reverend Peters, ain't I done warned you?" the woman said. "Ain't I done warned you? I said, ain't I done warned you, Reverend Peters?"

The old man acted as if he didn't even hear the woman. He sat there looking slyly at Phillip and smiling.

"I'm glad to have company," Phillip said.

"This ain't no church, Reverend Peters," the woman said. "How many times I done told you that? How many times, Reverend Peters?"

The old man ignored her. Phillip paid for the coffee and she went back behind the counter.

Peters laid his Bible on the table, and held his cup with both hands to drink his coffee. He set the cup back down and looked at Phillip.

"You look like a man of the Gospel?" he said.

Phillip nodded. "Yes."

"Not from round here though?"

"Across the river. St. Adrienne," Phillip said.

"Didn't get the name?"

"Phillip Martin."

"I see," Peters said.

He didn't know Phillip. He drank from his coffee, holding the cup with both hands as you would hold a chalice.

Phillip didn't like the way Peters looked at him from over the rim of the cup. He knew that Peters had been watching him a long time before coming to the table.

"You looking for somebody, ain't you?" Peters asked.

"Yes," Phillip said.

"I knowed it," Peters said. "A man of your quality don't sit in a place like this. This used to be a nice place, but no more. A few old people come in. Children sometime—but they don't respect nobody. No respect in children these days. And the old place going down, down, down."

"It still looks all right," Phillip said, and looked round the room. Everything in the room, from the hat and coat rack by the door to the chairs and tables all seemed too old and worn. Phillip noticed in several places where paint had peeled away from the walls.

"I reckon it's better than nothing, 'specially in weather like this," Peters said, looking round the room too. He looked at the things the way you look at them when you have seen them many, many times before. "But nothing like it used to be—nothing," he said, and looked at Phillip again. "I can remember when it was so nice, so nice. Who is it you looking for, if you don't mind me asking?"

Phillip started to say Chippo Simon, but he told Peters he was looking for his son.

"Live here in Baton Rouge?" Peters asked.

"I left him in St. Adrienne," Phillip said.

"And you looking—" he stopped.

He seemed to have some idea what Phillip was talking about. He covered Phillip's hand on the table with his own. The skin of his long brown fingers was the same color as the leather of his Bible, and just as wrinkled.

"He bothering you?" the woman asked from behind the counter.

"No," Phillip said.

"You better mind yourself there, Reverend Peters," the woman said. "I'm warning you."

Reverend Peters withdrew his hand.

"You asked Him to help you?" he asked Phillip.

"Yes," Phillip said, looking directly at Peters.

Peters saw something in Phillip's face that he didn't like. He started to speak but changed his mind. He looked down at the table and began drawing little marks on the cup with the tip of his finger. The marks he drew looked to Phillip like small crosses. He looked back at Phillip, his bloodshot eyes seeming even more watery now. He was trying to think of something encouraging to say.

"Sometime it takes time, time—years."

"Years?" Phillip said. "I don't have years. I don't even have days. We don't even have hours, Peters. We don't have any time at all."

"He will bring him back to you if you have faith," Peters said.

"Will He, Peters?"

Peters nodded his head. "If you have faith."

"Did you hear about the killing today?" Phillip asked.

"All Baton Rouge heard about it," Peters said.

"Sitting at the table eating," Phillip said. "Mama, brothers, sisters. Where was Turner?"

"They been separated."

"I picked up the papers the other day—yesterday, day before—I forget now. Story about a black boy frozen in a ditch of water. No papers. Nothing on him to tell who he was."

"Happens all the time," Peters said philosophically.

Phillip nodded. "Yes. All the time. Every day. About a month ago I was talking to a newspaper man—a man who's covered executions all over the South. Not just here in Louisiana—Texas, Mississippi, Georgia—all over. He's seen fifty, sixty of them. Most of them, black men. Said he never heard one called daddy's name at that last hour. Heard mama called, heard gran'mon, nanane—Jesus, God. Not one time he heard daddy called. Why not, Peters?"

"They called on God—that was good," Peters said.

" 'Daddy,' Peters. I'm saying 'daddy.' "

"He works in mysterious ways," Peters said. "Keep the faith, man. Never doubt."

"There's a gap between us and our sons, Peters, that even He," Phillip said, nodding toward the Bible, "even He can't seem to close."

"No such gap, man," Peters said, his watery eyes staring sadly at Phillip. "No such thing."

"He bothering you?" the woman asked, as if she had just wakened up and noticed that they were still there.

"We're just talking," Phillip said.

"You behave yourself there, Reverend Peters," the woman said.

"She's a good woman," Peters said to Phillip. "I'm cold, I come here; I'm hungry, I come here."

"It's good to have a friend—somewhere you can go—somebody you can talk to."

"We all have a friend," Peters said, and looked at his Bible. He looked at it a long time before turning back to Phillip. "We all have a friend," he said, nodding his head.

Phillip could see that he would not reach Peters no matter how much he tried to explain.

"I'm here to find a man named Chippo Simon," he said.

"I know Chippo Simon," Peters said.

"You seen him today?"

"Today? No. But I musta seen him yesterday. How can Chippo help you?"

Phillip shook his head. "It's a long, long story, Peters."

"You went by his house? You know where he lives?" Peters asked.

"I been there. He's not at home."

"You tried Jimmy's liquor store—Terrace and East Boulevard? He hangs round in there a lot."

"I haven't been there yet—I'll try it," Phillip said.

He drank the last of his coffee, then shook hands with Peters and stood up.

"Leaving?" the woman asked from behind the counter.

"Yes," Phillip said.

"Hope he didn't bother you too much."

"No bother at all," Phillip said. "I'm glad we met. Good night."

"Come back soon," the woman said. "Dettie cooks the best Creole food in town. Ask anybody."

Phillip promised her that he would. Driving back up the street, he thought he would go by Chippo's house again. He was hoping that he would not see the woman, but when he pulled up before the door he could see her standing behind the screen as if she had never moved.

"He ain't there," she said, when he got out of the car.

"I just want to leave him a note," Phillip told her.

He climbed the two steps up to the porch, and stuck the piece of paper in the crack of the door. On the paper, he had written: *Phil. Be back later.*

"You think he might be at Jimmy's liquor store?" he asked the woman.

"Good's any other place to look for him," she said. "Just tell him he better bring me my money on back here. I don't want have to call the law."

"How much does he owe you?" Phillip asked.

"He know," the woman said.

"I thought maybe I could pay you," Phillip said. He thought at least this would get the woman out of the cold.

"I don't want your money, I want my own," she said.

Phillip got back into his car and drove up to East Boulevard. He drove by the liquor store twice, trying to see through the glass door the people inside. After going by the second time he parked his car across the street so that he could watch the door. He was doubtful about going in there. This was a place where you not only bought your liquor, but where you drank it too. There would be men in there drinking, maybe even drunk, and anything could happen in a place like that. But if he didn't go in there, where else would he find Chippo? He knew him too well to go looking for him in church.

He sat watching the door. Each time the door opened, he could hear loud talking and laughing. After about ten minutes, he got out of the car and crossed the street.

The store was warm, crowded, noisy. Two youths played the pin ball machines against the wall. Another youth and an older man with a dead cigar stub in his mouth shot bumper pool on a table in the center of the room. The youth was beating the old man badly and teasing him. The old man pretended he didn't mind, but anyone watching the game could see that he was angry. Another group of men stood at the far end of the room. Most of the noise in the place came from that corner. Phillip could hear one man's shrill insistent voice above all the others. Then everyone would burst out laughing. The louder they laughed, the louder and more insistent the voice became. The louder he talked, the more uproariously the others laughed at him.

Other men stood at the counter drinking. One man or several would buy a half pint or a pint of whiskey, and the clerk behind the counter would serve them a pitcher of water and a bowl of ice with the bottle. Each man would then fix his own drink the way he wanted it.

No one paid any attention to Phillip when he first came into the store, and he moved closer to the counter and waited for one of the clerks to notice him. There were two clerks behind the counter. One was a tall, slim mulatto, who wore a clean white jacket. The other one was shorter, darker, and his white apron looked as if it belonged to a garage mechanic more than it did a bartender. Both of the clerks kept busy, serving and keeping the counter dry. At the same time, they laughed and joked with the other men at the far end of the room.

Phillip stood at the counter listening to the laughing and joking round him and remembered the many evenings when he and Chippo had done the same thing. He couldn't see too many changes between now and the way things were then. Maybe there were fancier lights and pictures on the jukebox and pin ball machines, and there were more black athletes and entertainers advertising beer and whiskey, but other than that he saw very few changes. Looking at the posters against the wall, he noticed one above the jukebox which he read to himself: NO WOMEN ALLOWED. BY ORDER OF THE HEALTH DEPARTMENT. Phillip smiled to himself and looked for other posters like this one, but there weren't any.

"Help you?" the clerk in the white jacket asked him.

"You Jimmy?" Phillip asked.

"Yeah, I'm Jimmy," the mulatto said.

"I'm looking for Chippo Simon," Phillip said. "Seen him around?"

Phillip used the same tone of language that he heard the others using round him.

"Chippo was in here earlier," Jimmy said. "Round two, I reckon. Ain't seen him since."

"You know where I might find him?" Phillip asked.

"You checked his house?"

"Yeah. He wasn't there."

"You tried next door? Wait." Jimmy turned from Phillip and called the other clerk. The clerk wearing the dirty apron came toward him with several empty beer cans which he threw in a garbage can under the counter. He then wiped his hand on the apron. "Little Man?" Phillip heard Jimmy asking him. "You know if Chippo still fucking that old gal—Alice Seaberry?"

"Last I heard," Little Man said.

Jimmy turned back to Phillip.

"Chippo got this old gal live next door to him, you tried her?"

"I talked to her. She didn't know where he was."

"Anybody round here know where Chippo went?" Jimmy

asked the men in the store. "Man here looking for Chippo Simon. Cue Stick, you was talking to Chippo—he told you were he was going?"

Cue Stick was the old man who was losing the pool game. He had been sighting at one ball the last couple of minutes. Now he stopped and looked back at Jimmy.

"Can't you not bother a man when he's gambling?" he said angrily.

"You ain't gambling, nigger, you getting a schooling," Jimmy said. "Anybody else in here seen Chippo? Frank, you seen Chippo?"

"I think him and California went cross the river," Frank said. Frank was a short dark man with a hoarse-sounding voice. He wore a derby over his shaven head. "If Chippo's got a dime, he'll be over there somewhere," he said.

"Anybody in here know if Chippo got any money?" Jimmy asked the men in the store.

"Had a few bucks on him this morning," someone else said at the counter. "Claimed some woman gived it to him."

"Best place to look for Chippo, cross the river," Jimmy said to Phillip. "Probably find him gambling over there somewhere."

"You wouldn't know where he gambles?" Phillip asked. "This is important."

"Don't some of y'all in here know where Chippo gambles?" the mulatto asked in a loud voice. "Sweet Brown, you gamble with Chippo and California all the time, tell the man here where they gamble."

Sweet Brown was tall and brown-skinned. He wore a brown cashmere overcoat, a brown hat, a brown suit, and his shirt and tie were also brown. He looked round slowly and shrugged his shoulders at Jimmy.

"Try 'em all," he said, gesturing with both hands. All his fingers had rings on them, and his fingernails were long and well manicured. "Try Hebert. Try Domico. Try Red Top.

Try Sill. Try any place that got a table—if Chippo got a dime."

"Or can borrow a dime—or steal one for that matter," Frank, wearing the derby, said.

"Chippo can be almost anywhere, mister," Jimmy said to Phillip. "No telling about Chippo Simon."

The group of men at the far end of the room burst out laughing again, and the one who had been talking loud moved away in disgust. He was short, thin, and very black. He wore khaki trousers, an Army field jacket, an Army field cap, and combat boots. When he got closer, Phillip could see that he was in his early or mid-twenties. His narrow, tight-skinned black face was shining with sweat, and there was a big scar across his left temple.

"Leaving us, Billy?" someone out of the crowd asked.

"Niggers will be niggers," Billy said.

The men laughed.

"Billy, don't leave," Jimmy said, from behind the counter. "Here, have a beer. One on the house. Little Man, get Billy a Falstaff out of there."

When Billy came up even with Phillip he stopped and shook his head.

"Niggers go'n be niggers. For the rest of they lives they go'n be niggers—you hear me?"

Phillip could see that Billy was angry, but he didn't know what to say to him. He didn't want to get into anything without knowing what it was all about.

"Here's your beer, Billy," Jimmy said. "Don't get mad; they just playing with you."

"That's niggers for you," Billy said to Phillip, not to Jimmy. "When they march them in the gas chamber niggers go'n still be just playing."

"Billy's trying to organize a little army round here," the man with the derby said. "Him and couple other boys been training round that bayou over there on Pichot Plantation.

Pichot catch you over there, he go'n shoot the hell out all of y'all."

"Go to hell, niggers," Billy said, and started toward the door. He pushed the door open but turned around and came back to the counter. "No, I don't mean that," he said seriously. "I don't mean that." He took the beer off the counter and drank. The men watched him and laughed. "Y'all my brothers," he said. "I must always remember that. Y'all still my brothers. I hope y'all wake up. Wake up, brothers, 'fore it's too late."

He finished drinking the beer and turned to leave.

"Have another one, Billy," Jimmy said.

"No, thanks," Billy said. "I got work to do."

"He's heading cross the river," Derby said. "Trying to recruit some more boys to go crawl round that bayou."

"You got a ride cross the river?" Jimmy asked Billy. "Man here going cross the river."

Billy had already pushed the door open. He let the door shut and came back to where Phillip was standing.

"You going toward Sun Rise?" he asked.

"I'm looking for Chippo Simon," Phillip said.

"He might be over there gambling," Billy said. "He gambles in Port Allen and Sun Rise."

"Be sure you take him to Hebert, not to Pichot Plantation," Derby said. "He want see Chippo, not crawl round that bayou."

A short yellowish man standing next to the derby man imagined Phillip crawling round the bayou and started laughing. He had just raised his drink to his mouth, but he started laughing so hard that he had to set the glass back down on the counter. He leaned on the counter laughing and shaking his head.

"That's right, keep on laughing," Billy said. "Keep on laughing. Don't organize. Laugh." He turned to Phillip. "You ready?"

"Don't go near Pichot with him," Derby told Phillip.

"He'll make you tie leaves all over your clothes, then run you through that bayou full speed—nothing but a stick for a gun."

The yellow man who was leaning on the counter raised one big hand up in the air, waved it round twice, and slammed it back down on the counter. He wanted to stop laughing, but the man wearing the derby wouldn't stop talking.

Billy asked Phillip again if he was ready to go, and they went out. The men were still laughing. Billy and Phillip could hear them laughing all the way to the car.

"Nobody laughs more than niggers," Billy said. "Nobody suffers more than niggers, nobody organize less than niggers—but nobody laughs more than niggers—nobody."

Phillip turned the car around and started toward the bridge that would take them out of Baton Rouge.

"What's this about Pichot Plantation?" he asked Billy.

"Me and some boys been meeting over there," Billy said. "I been teaching them guerrilla tactics."

"That's a dangerous game you playing there, Billy," Phillip said.

"Nobody's playing," Billy said.

"Even thinking about things like that can get a lot of people killed."

"In war people die," Billy said. "I was in Viet Nam. I know."

"It won't be war, it'd be suicide," Phillip told him.

"It's war if you plan it right," Billy said.

"Plan it right, how?" Phillip asked. "Where your guns, your tanks, your airplanes, your armies?"

"I don't need none of that."

"No?"

"They got twenty-five million black people in this country. All I need is a million for one day."

"A one-day war?" Phillip asked.

"One day."

"And how do you plan to win a one-day war?"

"Burning this country down."

"Burning it down?"

"To the level ground," Billy said.

"The white man's just go'n stand round with his hands in his pockets and let you burn this country down?"

"Nothing he could do about it," Billy said. "What could he do if all the fields and swamps caught fire at the same time one day? What could he do if every department store in a big city like New Orleans or New York or Atlanta caught fire at the same time one day? What could he do if ten, fifteen thousand gas pumps all waste gas at the same time, and somebody there to throw the match? The same thing for jails, the same thing for hospitals, schools, banks—we got people in all these places—what could he do if all this happened at three o'clock one hot summer day? Not a damn thing but watch it burn down. There ain't enough water on land to put out that kind of fire, and they damn sure can't use that much dynamite. It'll burn to the ground, and with that the honky'll cut his own throat. You wouldn't have to shoot him."

"And with that fire all over the place, where do your own people go?"

"We'll fight, and most of us'll die."

"And what have you won?"

"This country here is the last crutch for Western Civilization—what *they* call civilization," Billy said. "Burn it down, you destroy Western Civilization. You put the world back right—let it start all over again. Somebody got to pay for it, that's all."

"And you want us to do it?"

"We been giving our lifes for nothing all these years, we might as well die for something big. I don't mind putting mine on the line."

"And the rest of the people?"

"Some listening."

"And the others?"

"Laughing—like them old-ass niggers back there."

"You know why they're laughing, Billy?"

"No, I don't know why niggers always laughing," Billy said. "Any other race would be storming that fucking capital for what happened today."

"That young man who was killed?"

"That's who I'm talking about," Billy said. "They was sad about one hour—one hour. Now they in that goddamn liquor store drinking and laughing they ass off. Forgot about him already."

"They ain't forgot about him, Billy," Phillip said.

"That's a hell of a way to show the world they remember him."

"What else can they do, Billy? Tell me."

"Man, don't hand me that 'What else can they do?' shit," Billy said. "That's all I been hearing all my life. 'What else can poor niggers do? What else can poor niggers do?' If they stop grinning long enough they can organize themself—that's what they can do."

"A guerrilla army? That's the kind of organizing you mean?"

"Exactly."

"Get that out of your mind, Billy."

"Not in my lifetime."

"You go'n get yourself killed."

"Somewhere in the world people dying every day for changes," Billy said.

"You don't think your people have died here for changes?" Phillip asked him. "You don't see any changes your people have died for?"

"None," Billy said. "Niggers can vote. Vote for what? Voting can't fill your belly when you hungry. Another nigger sit up there in the capital. Doing what? Another one go to Washington. For what? They put another couple on television to broadcast news—them the changes you talking about? I'm talking about changes that keep white men from coming into South Baton Rouge and shooting down our people. If it happen, we pick up guns, we pick up torches, and we hit back. That's the changes I want to see."

"I pray we never have to pick up torches, or guns, Billy."

"I done forgot how to pray," Billy said.

"I hope you'll never have to strike that first match."

"I ain't hoping, neither; I'm planning on it." He looked at Phillip and grinned. But his eyes were deadly serious. "This little black ass nigger you see sitting here 'side you will one day destroy this world, Pops. We been here nearly four hundred years—nothing to show for it but pain and sorrow." He touched the big permanent scar across his left temple. "I got news for you, Pops, this world ain't going on like this much longer. This little black ass nigger you see sitting here 'side you go'n make sure of that. He go'n take one match—one match one day—and he go'n start the biggest revolution this world ever knowed. If I go with it, I go. If the world go with it, let the world go. Let the roaches have the ashes."

He lay his head back on the seat and shut his eyes. He was very tired. Phillip looked at his Army field clothes and at the big scar on his face. The scar was about the size of a two-inch-long pencil, and much lighter than the rest of his skin. Phillip wondered how Billy had been cut, but he wouldn't ask.

After keeping his eyes shut a few minutes, Billy raised his head from the back of the seat.

"You know, Chippo might not be over here," he said. "Much as he moves around."

"Maybe somebody'll know where he's at," Phillip said.

"Looking for him on a night like this, he must owe you some money."

"It's not money," Phillip said.

Billy looked at Phillip, waiting for him to go on.

"I want him to tell me about my oldest boy," Phillip said.

"In some kind of trouble?" Billy asked him.

Phillip nodded his head thoughtfully.

"What happened, Billy?" he said, turning to the young man beside him. "What ever happened between us?"

"I don't know what you mean," Billy said.

"You married?" Phillip asked him. "You got children?"

"No. I live with my mama and daddy."

"What's your daddy do?"

"Nothing much now. Semi-retired. Used to work at Standard Oil. Janitor."

"Y'all get along, you and your daddy, Billy?"

"I guess so. 'Bout average."

"What's average, Billy?"

"I don't bother him, he don't bother me."

"That's average?" Phillip asked him.

Billy shrugged his shoulders for the answer.

Phillip shook his head. "That's average? That's average?"

"Far as I'm concerned," Billy said. Then he said, "Better watch the road there, Pops."

"When did it happen?" Phillip asked, looking out on the road.

"When did what happen?" Billy asked.

"When did that gap come between you and your daddy?"

"I don't remember," Billy said.

"Not a particular day, not a particular thing?" Phillip asked.

"I don't remember no one day, no one thing," Billy said.

Phillip looked at him. "You mean we're born that way? The gap's already there when we take the first breath?"

"You getting a little deep for me," Billy said. "But you better watch the road. I don't want land in that ditch."

"How do we close the gap, Billy?" Phillip asked.

"I don't know," Billy said.

"The church?"

"Shit," Billy said, without hesitating a moment. "There ain't nothing in them churches, Pops, but more separation. Every little church got they own little crowd, like gangs out on the street. They all got to outdo the other one. Don't look for that crowd to close no gap."

"The whole civil rights program started in the church."

"Just because I can eat at the white folks' counter with my daddy, just because I can ride side him in the front of the bus don't mean we any closer," Billy said.

"Then the civil rights movement didn't bring us together at all?"

"Not that I can see," Billy said.

"Then what will close the gap between you and your daddy, between me and my boy?"

"My daddy got to catch up with me," Billy said. "I can't go back where he's at."

"You mean pick up a match?"

"If that's what it come to."

"I don't think he can do that, Billy."

"And I sure can't become a janitor, mister," Billy said. "I see what it can do to you. At forty-five a massive heart attack. Frustrated over all the things you wanted to be but couldn't be. I'm twenty-four now. When I'm forty-four I'll be dead or free. But I won't be part of the living dead."

"Your daddy, me, we're the living dead?"

"No more than I am, mister," Billy said. "I just don't plan to be it all my life."

They were coming up to Hebert's, and Billy nodded for Phillip to pull off the highway. Hebert's was no more than a cabin with beer, cigarette, and cold drink signs nailed against the wall. Cars driving up to the front door and backing away had dug ruts into the gravel, and the holes were filled with water. Two or three cars were parked before the door now. Billy told Phillip that he would go inside to see if Chippo was in there. Phillip could hear the music from the jukebox when Billy opened the door. A minute later he heard the music again when Billy came back out. No, Chippo wasn't there, but he might show up any time.

"They don't know for sure?" Phillip asked.

"Not with Chippo," Billy said.

"Any other places round here he gambles?"

"I don't know of any right here in Sun Rise," Billy said. "Got a couple back up the road there in Port Allen."

"What they got in there to eat?" Phillip said, nodding toward the door of the nightclub.

"Pig feet," Billy said. "Crackling. Pig lips."

Phillip frowned and shook his head. "None of that."

"Good food at Red Top, if you want drop in there," Billy said.

Phillip nodded agreeably. "I used to go there years, years ago," he said. "You think Chippo might be there?"

"They gamble there; anywhere they gamble you might find him," Billy said. "I brought you here first because this where he hangs out most on this side the river. But anywhere you can find a table . . ."

"You want me to drop you off anywhere?" Phillip asked.

"No, I'm go'n hang around here a while," Billy said. "Some boys in here I want talk to."

Phillip looked closely at him. "Be careful, Billy," he said.

"You got to take some chances," Billy said.

"Chances like that can get you in a lot of trouble."

Billy grinned. "Mister, I been through hell. Nothing scares me no more. I know I got to take chances. But that's the only way you get things done. You know any other way?"

"No," Phillip said. "But it's the aim you have in mind."

"No more than what that honky's got in mind," Billy said. "You don't think that honky got genocide in mind?"

"I don't know that," Phillip said.

Billy tapped the side of his head. "I do know that," he said. He leaned on the car and looked at Phillip a moment before going on. "You see all them empty fields round here, mister?" he asked. "Go all over this place—empty fields, empty houses, empty roads. Where the people used to be—nothing. Machines. Every time they build another machine that takes work from the people, they hire another hundred cops to keep the people quiet. Oh, they let a black slip in here, slip in there every now and then, but for every one that get a little position they hire another hundred cops to keep the rest back. That's why they killed Hal today. They didn't kill Hal for the food he took. Niggers steal food like that all day long. Them honkies know it; they see them doing it. They don't do nothing but cheat the next man who come along. Hal wasn't killed because of sausage and bread, he was killed because he was one of my boys. Killed because we been hollering. Hollering about how they work you for nothing, how they cheat you, how they make you pay for third-rate food. Food they can't sell in other stores, they bring here in South Baton Rouge and sell to the niggers. They killed Hal to shut him up; they killed him to shut me up. Well, they ain't shutting nobody up. They just go'n make us work harder."

"Hard work, yes," Phillip said. "But what kind of hard work?"

"The honky don't understand but two things, mister—bullets and fire. This whole country's been built on bullets and fire. Go ask the Indians, go ask the Japs. Go ask the Koreans, the Vietnamese. All nonwhite people. Even when they lynch a nigger they have to burn him too. Bullet and fire is all he knows. Well, I intend to get there first."

Phillip took a deep breath. He felt very tired. He was too tired to make a comment, too tired to ask another question. He glanced at the scar but wouldn't ask about it either.

Billy touched the scar with his finger. "Got them like that all over my body," he said. "A grenade. Six of us. I was the only one got out. My best friend got it. Boy from Detroit. Sweetest old boy you ever seen. Named Boopy Scott. Ugly—

good Lord, that nigger was ugly—but funny as hell. Always making people laugh. Had a' Indian boy there from California. A Catholic. One of the nicest people in the world. Never knowed a' Indian could be a Catholic. Not the shit they done took from people claim to be Christians. Had a' Italian boy there too. Couple other boys from the Midwest. All of them got it but me."

Phillip could see in Billy's face the love he had for his dead comrades. He could detect the sorrow in his voice as he talked about them.

"God spared you for a reason, Billy," he said.

"I got out of there, mister, because I had the best shelter," Billy said. "If you think I can thank God for saving me and letting my boys go like that you crazy. Well, I'm getting a little cold, I better go inside. Thanks a lot for the ride."

He straightened up from the car and turned to leave. He had gone a couple of steps when Phillip called him back. Phillip was very tired, but he wanted to say one last thing.

"God spared you for a reason," he said. "You a bright young man, a brave young man. Use your talent well to help your people. Nothing good will come out of that idea you have in mind."

Billy leaned on the car again.

"Mister," he said. "My boys all died. Boopy died. Jerry died. Manny died. Jim died. Hal died today. All of them fought for this country—all of them dead. For what? For nothing. Nothing changed. Detroit ain't changed, Chicago ain't changed, California, neither South Baton Rouge. Nothing go'n change till somebody change it."

He stood away from the car, saluted Phillip, then turned and went back into the bar.

Phillip sat there a moment watching the door. He wondered what else he could have said to Billy to make him change his mind. He could see that he was a determined young man, and he knew he should have said something else to him—but what? What advice could he have given him? What had he to offer Billy in place of what the world had already done to him?

He started back up the road toward the Red Top Saloon. He was still thinking about Billy, comparing him to his own son in St. Adrienne. They were about the same age, and they were saying practically the same thing. There were probably many others just like them. He saw it in some of the younger schoolteachers in St. Adrienne. They could not say in public the things that Billy and his son could say, but by their actions they showed that they felt the same way about God, Law, and Country. He asked himself how would he ever reach them—could he ever reach them?

Five minutes after he left Billy, he pulled up in front of the Red Top Saloon. Red Top was a square, white, stucco building with a red door facing the street. Over the door was a yellow light, the bulb so covered with grime that it gave only a dull glow. There were other cars parked on the gravel in front and to the left of the building. Farther to the right was a garage where Phillip could hear men talking. To the left was a grocery store, and on the opposite side of the street was a line of houses, separated from the road by a ditch of water.

Phillip didn't get out of the car for a while. He felt strange being in front of the saloon, and he knew he would feel even more strange inside. But what else could he do? If he wanted Chippo, he had to look for him. Still he sat there, watching the door, waiting, hoping that someone would come out that he might ask if Chippo was in there. But no one did, and he had to go in for himself.

The place was dimly lighted, crowded, and noisy, but still lighted enough so that Phillip could see that not too many changes had been made since the last time he was in there. The only big change that he noticed were the people. They were younger; they could have been the children of the ones he had drunk and gambled with. But everything else was much the same as it was fifteen, twenty, even more years back than that. The ceiling was always painted that same blood-red color—just as the door was—and so low that a man his size could touch it just by raising his arm. The bar looked the same, with its familiar jars of pig feet and pickled sausage, and cracklings in greasy paper bags. You still got the odor of fried fish and fried chicken mixed with the odor of alcohol, because ever since Julian Ferdinand had the place twenty, twenty-five years ago there had always been a kitchen in back. The floor was muddy now, just as it had always been in winter. The jukebox was one of the newer ones with fancy lights and pictures, but it sat practically in the same place as the old one did. The tables were covered with red-and-white checkered oilcloth. Two young waiters in white jackets, with their dish towels over their shoulders or across their arms, went from the bar to the tables, to the food counter in back. Nothing had changed here—nothing; except that most of the people in here now were only half Phillip's age.

A small, light-brown-skinned woman behind the bar noticed that he had come in, and she came to the end of the bar to see what he wanted. She was about the same age as the rest of the people in the place.

"I'm looking for Chippo Simon," Phillip told her. "I heard he comes in here."

"Haven't seen him today," the woman said. "He might drop in later."

"They still gamble round the other side?" Phillip asked.

"Game going on right now."

"Who runs the table?"

"Waco."

"I don't think I know him," Phillip said.

"Been with us about a year now," the woman said. "Don't think I ever seen you round here before, but look like I know your face from somewhere."

"I haven't been here in a long time," Phillip said. "Fifteen years."

"That's been too long," the woman said, smiling at him. "You shouldn't stay 'way like that."

Phillip smiled back.

"Get you something to drink?" she asked him.

"No, I think I'll get something from the kitchen."

"In the back," she said, nodding.

"Yes, I know," Phillip said.

He started to walk away.

"You want to leave your name—for Chippo?" the woman asked him.

"Tell him Phil," Phillip said.

"No last name?"

"He'll know," Phillip said.

"All right, old 'He'll know,'" the woman said, flirting with him still.

Phillip started for the kitchen again. Someone had started a record on the jukebox, and several people moved out on the floor to dance.

Phillip ordered a chicken dinner at the kitchen counter. The short dark woman behind the counter, wearing a white dress and an apron, asked him if he were going to eat in there. He told her no. But he had said it too quickly, and she didn't like the sound of it. She looked him over closely—the overcoat, the suit, the hat. No one else in the place was dressed quite like him—and perhaps he thought he was too good to eat in there with the rest. Phillip could see how the woman felt, and he wanted to apologize, but he didn't know how.

"Food go'n take a while," she said, and turned away.

Phillip stood at the counter watching the dancers. The jukebox against the wall, with its bright red, green, and yellow lights, played a slow tempo blues by BB King. The dancers held each other close, hardly moving their feet at all, only their bodies keeping time with the beat of the music. Phillip could remember when he had danced here.

Not to BB King's records, but to Louis Jordan's, Joe Turner's, and some of the other earlier blues singers.

Phillip noticed a woman sitting at a table watching him. She was very light-skinned and dressed entirely in red—red hat, red dress, with a red overcoat hanging on the back of her chair, and a red patent-leather pocketbook lying on the table in front of her. There was a bottle of whiskey on the table, a pitcher of water, a bowl of ice, two glasses—but the woman sat alone. Phillip nodded to her, and she smiled and nodded back. He thought she reminded him of someone he had known years ago, but she sat too far away from the counter, and too much in the dark, and he couldn't see her face well enough to be sure.

He turned, and now he could see the door that led into the gambling room. He wondered if Chippo could have come in through the back and gone into the room without the bartender seeing him. He told the woman in the kitchen that he would be back later to get his food. She didn't answer, she didn't even look around.

For a moment, after he came up to the door, Phillip would not go into the room where the men were shooting dice. But dressed as he was he knew it didn't look right standing back, and he moved farther inside. About half a dozen men stood round the old green-flannel-covered table, and about that many stood back watching the game. The boy with the dice couldn't have been more than fifteen years old. He shook them closer to his ear, then slammed them against the table wall. Someone gathered them up and threw them back to him. He rubbed them together in the palms of his hands, blew his breath on them, shook them close to his ear again, and threw them back cross the table.

"Dollar say you can't nine, Po Boy," a big gambler with a white cowboy hat said.

Po Boy dropped a wrinkled dollar bill on the table. The bill was so wrinkled, so old, it would be impossible to ever smooth it out again. Phillip recognized the dollar bill, just as he recognized Po Boy as himself.

Eight came up on his next throw. Somebody tossed them back at him. He gathered them up with a small, hardened black hand, blew on them, rattled them against his ear, and grunted out loud as he slammed them against the wall while calling on God for help.

Six popped up.

"That's right, flirt with death, nigger," the man in the white hat said.

Phillip turned to leave. He had looked closely at the men in the room, and Chippo was not in there.

"Taking off, Big Man?" White Hat asked him.

"I was looking for Chippo Simon."

"Stick around, he might drop in."

"Tell him Phil was looking for him."

"Sure, Big Man," White Hat said.

The woman had his dinner ready when he came back to the counter. The dinner was a dollar and a half, and he gave her two dollars and told her to keep the change. As he turned to leave, he saw the woman in red who had been watching him earlier raise her glass and nod to him. He went to the table.

"Don't tell me you don't recognize me?" she said.

"Adeline Toussaint?"

"Nobody else."

"Not Adeline Toussaint?" he said.

"That's right," she said and smiled.

She was a very handsome woman, with high cheekbones, large dark-brown eyes, and full lips. The brim of her big red hat turned up on one side. She had a small dark mole just above the left corner of her mouth. She and Phillip had been lovers once. A sudden warm good feeling came over him that he wished was not there.

"Sit down," she said.

"How about your friend?"

"He's gambling."

"He won't mind?"

"He's gambling."

He sat down opposite her and set his paper plate of food on the table. She was looking at him and smiling.

"How many years?" he asked her.

She shrugged her shoulders. "Fifteen—something like that."

"About fifteen," he said. "And you haven't changed a bit in all that time. How'd you do it?"

"The best whiskey," she said, smiling and looking at him closely. "Look like you put on a little round the middle there."

"Yes," he said, and patted his stomach.

"I been reading about you," she said. "Seen you on the television, far away as New Orleans."

"You been living in New Orleans?"

"New Orleans, Houston, New York, California a while. Even Paris."

"All them places didn't do you no harm."

"I make out all right."

"Yes," he said, looking at her admiringly, and remembering the way things had been between them, and feeling a way now that he knew was not right.

"Fix you a drink?" she asked him.

"No," he said.

"Perfectly all right."

"No," he said.

She raised her glass and drank, watching him all the time.

"How is your family?" she asked him.

"Fine."

"When did you get married?"

"Not long after we split up."

"I was shocked when I heard it. Never thought you would. Never thought you'd get religion either."

"It was about time for both," Phillip said.

"Oh, I don't know about that. You were still pretty wild."

"I was getting pretty old, too."

"Nothing get old but clothes," she said. "What in the world you doing in a nightclub, and of all places Red Top?"

"I might ask you the same thing," Phillip said. "After New York, Paris, California?"

"Adeline drifts with the wind," she said. "Adeline wears red. You wear black."

"I'm looking for Chippo," Phillip said.

"Chippo back in these parts?" she asked. "I haven't seen Chippo—God knows—ten, eleven years. Is he back around here?"

"Staying in Baton Rouge," Phillip said. "Just got back from California. Saw my children out there."

"I didn't know you had children in California. Grown children?"

"My oldest boy nearly thirty," he said.

"Didn't know that," Adeline said. "Didn't know you had been married before."

"No, we never got married," he told her. "And yourself?"

"Married twice. Never lasted. No children."

"That's too bad."

"What?"

"Neither of your marriages lasted."

"They wanted something I couldn't give."

He looked at her, waiting.

"Love," she said.

He looked deeply into her eyes, and she looked directly back at him. She drank and set her glass back down. She was still looking at him.

"Love?" he said.

She nodded her head.

"Why did you get married?"

"They wanted to."

"Both times?"

She nodded again.

"But you did love once?"

"Did I?"

"You said so."

She laughed. "Stop it, Phillip Martin."

He was hurt. "Well?"

"How many times that's been said by both man and woman? How many times you yourself have said that to a woman? You meant it every time?"

His feelings were hurt still. He shook his head. "No."

"A woman can lie too—in more ways than one."

"Were you lying all the time, Adeline?"

"With you?"

"Yes."

"No."

"That Mardi Gras day in your sister's house when it was raining? The rain beating on the roof?"

She thought back. "Not that day," she said. She smiled to herself. "Even now I can remember that day. No, that day I was definitely not lying. What a day. Mardi Gras has never been the same.

"On the Bayou Goulah, the old man's place? That little cabin by the church?"

"Let me see, let me see, that little cabin by the church? That little cabin by the church? Oh yes, yes, now I remember. Yes, I was lying that day."

"Do you remember that dance right here at Red Top when Wyonnie Harris played till daybreak?"

"We danced here many times."

"I had a little Ford then, a little gray Ford."

"I remember that little car."

"Were you lying when I took you home that morning?"

She looked up at the ceiling as if she was trying to recall what had happened. Her eyes narrowed, her mouth opened slightly as if she was in deep thought. He looked at her, thinking how beautiful she still was. She was forty, but she could have easily passed for thirty, thirty-two. He watched her as she looked back at him nodding her head. "Yes, I was lying that morning."

"I think you're lying now," he told her. "I think you loved me that morning, you loved me all them other mornings. You left me because you was scared I might leave you. That was it, wasn't it, Adeline?"

"If that's what you want to believe," she said.

"That's what I believe," he said. "You wasn't the one lying, Adeline, it was me all the time. I'm wondering now, after all these years, if I'm not still lying. Lying to myself. God. Lying to my people."

"I don't follow you. What are you saying, Phillip?"

He looked across the table at her. She could see the agony in his face.

"I'm at war with myself, Adeline. I'm at war with my soul. For the past few days I've been questioning myself. I come up with nothing but doubts—about everything."

She didn't like the way he was talking. She wanted to do something. She wanted to touch his face. But she touched his hand instead. He drew his hand away from her. He didn't like the way her touch made him feel.

"Let me fix you a drink," she said.

"Make it thin. Very thin."

After fixing the drink she tasted it to see if it was all right. Her full red lips lingered on the glass a while before she passed it back to him. She fixed another drink for herself.

"Here's to you," she said. They touched glasses, and she looked over her glass at him while she drank.

"You want to talk?" she asked him.

He shook his head. "I'm very tired. But I have to find Chippo."

"That can take all night, looking for somebody like Chippo."

"You probably right. I ought to go back to his house and wait. He's got to show up there sometime."

"Why go back there?" she said. "Why not wait at my sister's house? I'm sure I could make it more comfortable for you there."

"That's no good, Adeline."

"No. Since when?"

"Look around this place."

He watched her as she looked across the room.

"What do you see?"

"People," she said.

"Half our ages," he told her.

"Well?" she said, looking at him. "What does that mean?"

"Just something I shoulda done when I was that age," he said. "And I wouldn'ta been here tonight."

"Could you've done it at that age?"

"I don't know," he said.

"I do know," she told him. "No."

He finished his drink and got up from the table with his plate of food. "It was nice seeing you again, Adeline," he said. "Take care yourself."

"I'll be going back to my sister's house in a few minutes," she said. "In case you change your mind, look in the phone book, under Louise Richard. I'll be there, waiting."

"Good bye, Adeline," Phillip said to her.

She raised her glass to him. But she didn't say good bye.

10

When Chippo came into the room, he saw Phillip asleep in a chair by the heater. His overcoat was on the sofa against the wall, and his hat was on top of the coat. Chippo laid his own hat and coat on the sofa, then he pulled up a chair to sit and watch Phillip. His bad eye was toward him, so he had to swing the chair around more in order to see him better.

Chippo was a tall, slim, but solidly built man in his early sixties. His long, narrow face was the color of dark, well-used leather, and it looked just as tough. His sharp features, his thick, curly black-gray hair showed that he had as much white or Indian in him as he did African. He looked like a person who did not worry much; he would take life as it came. As he watched Phillip he was continuously rubbing his left index finger over his bottom lip. He knew why Phillip was there. He knew that Phillip had heard from someone else that he had seen Johanna in California, and now Phillip wanted him to talk about it. He wished now that he hadn't come back to Louisiana. He didn't want to talk about what he had seen and heard.

He remembered that he had a bottle of whiskey in the

kitchen, and he went back there to get a drink. He couldn't find a single glass that wasn't dirty, and after rinsing out two in the sink he returned to the front. Phillip was awake when he came back. For a moment they only looked at each other. Chippo had the wet glasses in one big hand, and the bottle of whiskey in the other. He looked and felt uncomfortable. Phillip looking up at him with bloodshot eyes seemed tired and worried.

"Chippo," he spoke.

Chippo smiled and nodded his head. "How are you, man?"

Phillip stood up. He was much heavier than Chippo, but not quite as tall. Chippo set the glasses and bottle on the floor, and he and Phillip shook hands. Then they both sat down, and Chippo poured whiskey into each glass. He handed Phillip one of the glasses, but Phillip shook his head. Chippo looked around for a place to set the glass and finally placed it on the arm of Phillip's chair.

"I got little coffee back there," he said. "Just need to warm it up."

"No," Phillip said. He was very tired, and he wanted to get back home. He could tell by Chippo's face that Chippo knew why he was there, and waited for Chippo to start talking.

"How you been?" Chippo asked him.

"All right," Phillip said.

"Put on little weight there, I notice," Chippo said.

"Yes," Phillip said, looking at him and waiting for him to start talking.

"Me, myself, I stay the same," Chippo said, and slapped his flat, hard stomach. "Not an ounce."

He drank from his glass and looked down at the heater. Phillip was still looking at him and waiting. Chippo could feel it on the side of his face.

"How's the folks?" he asked Phillip.

"Everybody's fine, Chippo," Phillip said.

From the tone of his voice, Chippo could tell that Phillip didn't want to talk about the folks here. But Chippo didn't want to talk about the ones in California either.

"I have to get down there and see them sometime," he said. "When the last time you seen the old place?"

"Today," Phillip said. "I talked to Louis."

"Louis?" Chippo asked.

"Louis Patin." Phillip said.

For a moment Chippo still didn't understand what he meant. But as he and Phillip continued looking at each other, he remembered that he had seen Louis in Jimmy's liquor store only a few days ago. He remembered that he and someone else were talking about California and he mentioned the names of some of the people that he had seen out there. He had only casually mentioned Johanna's name, and that was by accident. Louis must have overheard it.

"Well?" Phillip said.

Chippo took a quick drink. He didn't feel like talking about what he had seen and heard. This was why he had not gone to St. Adrienne to see Phillip, or to Reno Plantation to visit the old people. He knew they would have asked him a lot of questions, and he probably would have said things that he wished he didn't know anything about.

"I know you saw her," Phillip said. "Did you see the children too?"

"Just one," Chippo said, nodding his head but not looking at Phillip. Then suddenly he stopped and shook his head. "No, no, I didn't see him, I heard him."

"Which one?" Phillip asked.

"The oldest one. Etienne."

Phillip moaned deep in his chest and covered his face with both hands. Chippo jerked up his head to look at him.

"Something the matter?" he asked.

Phillip shook his head, his face still covered. Chippo thought he knew why.

"Well, it's been a long time," he said.

Phillip drew his hands down slowly. He was looking toward Chippo, but not directly at him. He was ashamed to look directly at him.

"The others?" he said.

"Antoine and Justine?"

Phillip nodded his head. "Yes," he said. "Etienne, Antoine, and Justine."

"It's been a long time," Chippo said.

"Yes, a long time," Phillip said.

Chippo took a big drink and looked down at the heater. He was really sorry now that he had come back here. For a while neither one of them said anything else. The house was so quiet, it seemed that no one was in there. But Chippo knew that Phillip was sitting only a couple of feet away from him, and he knew that Phillip was watching him again.

"You said you didn't see any of the children?"

"No. I just heard Etienne in the room."

"You never seen him, not once?"

"No. He stayed in that room all the time."

"And the other two—Antoine and Justine?"

"They had gone," Chippo said.

"Gone where?"

"To the North. I think she said New York. Somewhere out that way."

Phillip watched him in silence a while. Chippo could feel it.

"What happened out there, Chippo?" he asked.

Chippo had been staring down at the heater all the time, but now he raised his head.

"What you mean?"

"What happened out there in California?"

"Nothing I know of," Chippo said.

"You know all right," Phillip said. "You know a lot. And I want to know too, Chippo."

"Know what, man?"

"About my other two children," Phillip said. "About Johanna. My other two children, they live or dead, Chippo?"

"I just said they was living in New York."

"Why did they go to New York, Chippo?"

"Why? I don't know why. Tired of Frisco, I reckon."

"That's a lie, Chippo, and you know it," Phillip said.

Chippo drank from his glass and looked at Phillip with his one good eye. Phillip was waiting. Chippo sighed deeply, resignedly.

"She told me not to tell it," he said.

"Not to tell what?"

"About the children."

"What happened to the children, Chippo?"

Chippo nodded toward Phillip's glass on the arm of the chair, but Phillip wouldn't look at the glass. Chippo leaned forward from his chair and poured himself another drink from the bottle on the floor.

"Well, Chippo?" Phillip said.

"Why don't you have a drink, man?" Chippo said. "It'll make me feel better."

Phillip didn't even look at the glass. "Well?" he said.

"I don't want talk about it," Chippo said.

"You will talk, Chippo, before I leave from here," Phillip said. "What didn't she want me to know about my children?"

Chippo shook his head. "It wasn't her. She was too 'shamed of it. The old man who runned the store, he was the one."

"What did he tell you, Chippo—so shameful she didn't want me to know about?"

"Have a drink, man," Chippo said. "Old Foster never killed nobody."

Phillip raised the glass but barely let it touch his lips. He was looking at Chippo and waiting.

"Johanna still love you, Phillip," Chippo said.

"I still love her."

Chippo grunted and looked at Phillip accusingly. "No, no," he said. "You don't love her that way." He touched his chest with his glass. "Deep, deep love for you. Up till a month ago, she thought you might knock on that door any moment to take her back."

"After twenty years?" Phillip asked.

"Up to a month ago she still thought so."

"Is she all right?" Phillip asked.

"You mean is she crazy?"

He didn't say it. But Chippo could see that's what he meant.

"No," Chippo said, shaking his head. "She ain't crazy. Not crazy at all. Some people just hope forever."

"But all that time, Chippo. No word. No letters. Nothing."

"At first I couldn't believe it either," Chippo said. "I kept telling myself, 'No, no, no.' But it was there. It was there, all right."

He drank.

"Y'all talked, and you told her about me?" Phillip asked.

"She asked about you," Chippo said. "I told her. That was before I knowed how she felt. I told her you was married, you had a family, you was preaching in St. Adrienne."

"Etienne was there when you told her this?"

"In that room—yes."

"So that's how he found out where I was," Phillip said to himself.

"Who?" Chippo asked.

"Etienne."

Chippo had been looking at Phillip from the side. But now he swung his chair round to face him directly.

"He's here?"

"Been in St. Adrienne over a week now," Phillip said.

"What—he come to see you?"

"He wanted to kill me. When he heard where I was he went to her and told her he wanted to kill me."

"That boy's crazy," Chippo said. "Not her. Him. He's the one crazy."

"I don't doubt it," Phillip said. "I don't doubt it at all. But something drove him crazy. What drove him crazy, Chippo? What she didn't want me to know about?"

Chippo turned his head to keep from looking at him. "The girl was raped," he said. "Antoine killed the man." He drank quickly after saying it.

Phillip's whole body sank further down into the chair. Etienne had described the rape and killing that morning, but he didn't know whether he could believe him or not. He could have been saying it just to hurt him more. But Phillip knew Chippo had no reason to lie.

"She come through it all right," Chippo said, looking back at him. "Married. Living in New York with her husband and children."

"And the boy?" Phillip asked.

"They gived him five years," Chippo said. "He's out now."

"That was 'leven years ago?"

"Yes. 'Bout 'leven years ago," Chippo said.

"Something else happened in that house during that time, Chippo. What was it? Why they both left home?"

"I don't know," Chippo said.

"Today he told me his brother and sister was both dead."

"He told you a lie," Chippo said. "They living in New York."

"I didn't finish," Phillip said. "He said they was dead to him and his mama. What he meant by that, Chippo? I want to know. I have to know everything."

Chippo looked at him painfully a long time. He didn't feel like talking, but he knew he had to. He took another drink, a big one. He coughed twice. Phillip was watching him and waiting.

"I had just come in from Seattle—visiting my sister

Mildred and her husband there in Frisco," he began. "I know lot of people all over that West Coast from my Merchant Marine days, and whenever I go out there I'm always hopping from one place to the other. One day I got on the bus to go visit an old white seaman we have there in the Marine hospital. I'm sitting there thinking about the old seaman, all them days we shipped together, when I see this woman stand up and get off the bus. I don't pay her too much attention at first, but after she start walking up the block, I think to myself I must know that woman there. But it just don't come to me that can be Johanna. The woman is too old to be Johanna. I go, sit, talk with the old seaman couple hours, then go on back to Mildred's place. All this time I'm still thinking 'bout that woman on the bus. When Mildred and her husband come in from work I ask her if she know if Johanna Martin live here in Frisco. She say, no, she don't know. I told her I was almost sure that that woman I had seen was Johanna. The only thing that held doubt in my mind was that the woman looked too old to be Johanna. Johanna was much younger than me; this woman looked much older. I told her I was going back. She told me 'fore I did I ought to look in the telephone book to see if I could find her name. We looked under Martin, we looked under Rey. Nothing. Mildred's husband gived me his car keys and I drove back to where I had seen her get off the bus. I asked everybody I met if they knowed a Johanna Martin or a Johanna Rey. Nobody knowed a thing. Then I went in a little corner store owned by an old black couple. I find out they from Texas, I'm from Louisiana, so we start talking. Just me and the husband at first, his wife was still upstairs. After we had been talking a little while, I asked about Johanna. At first he make 'tend he don't know who I'm talking 'bout. But when I tell him I been knowing her all my life—least till she left the South—he come out and tell me he know her very well. Just about then his wife come downstairs, and he tell his wife I've been asking 'bout Johanna.

The old lady looked at me the same way he did at first—like she don't want talk about it. I had to tell her, just like I told him, how long I had knowed Johanna. I told her about you, I told her about the three children, I told her about the people back here. 'They live up the street there,' she told me. She told me what the house looked like, she didn't know the number, but she told me it wouldn't be hard to find. I thanked them and started to leave. I got almost to the door, and the old man stopped me. 'We didn't send you there,' he said. 'You just stumbled on the place. They don't like no visitors.' 'Her and her husband?' I asked him. The old man grunted and looked at his wife. 'Husband,' he said to her. 'Husband. That's funny, ain't it?' The old lady didn't answer him, just looking at me all the time. 'Him,' he said to me. 'Him?' I asked. 'Him,' he said again. I thought him and his little wife was acting a little crazy, and I thanked them again and left.

"Johanna didn't live a block from the store, in the basement of one of these big old three-story buildings. She answered the door soon as I knocked. But I couldn't believe it was her. Her hair was grayer than mine is now. She had lost teeth. Her skin loose, sagging. She looked ten, fifteen years older than she ought to be.

" 'Chippo?' she said. 'Chippo Simon? Lord have mercy, if it ain't Chippo Simon.'

" 'Yes,' I said.

"She throwed her arms round me, hugging me, then she stood back wiping her eyes. 'Chippo. Chippo Simon,' she kept on saying.

" 'Yes, it's me,' I said.

"Then I caught her looking toward the door. I thought she was looking for the person who had brought me there. But I know now she was looking for you. Her mind was still locked on how we used to travel together years, years ago. When you saw one, you saw the other. And she just figured that the both of us was together this time too.

"We stood there talking in the front room a while, then she invited me back in the kitchen for some coffee. We had to go through her bedroom, then pass another little room on the left 'fore you reached the kitchen. None of the rooms was too big, but in that kitchen you felt like you was in a box. The ceiling was just a few inches over my head, and no matter where you stood in there you could touch one side of the wall. I sat down at the table, and she went to the stove to warm the coffee. She never quit talking all the time she was over there.

"She wanted to know everything. How was the old place? Had it changed much? How was the people? Who was still there? Was so and so still there? Was the church still there? Was the graveyard still there? Was the people still farming? What did they grow in the fields now? Did they still fish out there in the river.

"She brought the coffee to the table and sat down, but I did all I could to keep from looking straight at her. It hurt me to see her like this. 'Cause I could remember how pretty she was when she left from here. She went on talking and talking. I played round with my hat, I grinned a lot, and kept my eyes down. But she was so glad to see me, she never noticed I wasn't looking at her.

"After a while the talk came round to you. When was the last time I had seen you? I told her. And what was you doing now? I told her preaching. She couldn't believe it. She said it over and over. Preaching? Preaching? Phillip Martin preaching? Then she started laughing. Laughed and laughed and laughed.

" 'Lord, have mercy,' she said. 'Will miracles never end? I reckon he's got lots and lots of girlfriends? Preachers, you know, always got to have the girls round them.'

"I told her no, no more girlfriends; you was married now, wife and children. And soon as I said it I seen it was a trap she had been setting all the time. Just like that it got quiet. No more laughing now, no more talking—quiet.

To say you had girlfriends was one thing; you had always had lots of girlfriends, and you was always leaving them. But to say you had a wife, children, and settled down was the last thing in the world she ever wanted to hear. It was quiet now—quiet, quiet. The little happiness I'd brought for a moment was gone now—gone for good.

" 'Who?' she said.

"I didn't look at her. I couldn't look at her. All I wanted was to get out of there and get out of Frisco.

" 'Who?' she said.

"I looked down at my old hat, touching it here, touching it there.

" 'Chippo, who?' she said.

"I told her.

" 'She was a child when I left from there,' she said. 'Not much older than my oldest boy. You sure that's the one, Chippo?'

"I didn't answer her. I just wanted to get out of there. A minute later I told her I had to meet somebody. I didn't have nobody to meet. All I was go'n do was go back to Mildred's place and sit there with her and her husband and drink. But I didn't care what I did, long as I got away from that house.

"She wanted to know when I was heading back this way. I shoulda told her I was leaving first thing in the morning, but, me, no, I told her I wouldn't be leaving till that weekend. That was Tuesday. Now she told me she wanted me to come take dinner with her Thursday 'fore I left. Me, 'fore I knowed what I was saying, I'm telling her I would.

"We had smothered beef shank, rice, mustard greens, and cornbread. Cake and coffee for dessert. I was sitting cross the table from her, and for no reason at all—no reason I can tell—she all a sudden raised her head and looked toward the door behind my back. What got her 'tention? I don't know. She remembered something? I don't know that either. Heard something? I don't know—'cause I sure hadn't heard a thing. But since they had been there all them years by themself, maybe they had a way of sig'ling each other 'thout nobody else knowing. Anyhow, next thing I know, she asking me: 'Where you say he was?' We hadn't mentioned your name at all that day, but she couldn'ta been talking 'bout nobody else but you. I told her, 'St. Adrienne.'

"That's when I heard the noise—the bed. I had thought all the time it wasn't nobody in the house but me and her. I know the storekeeper had told me about a 'him' who stayed there with her, but I hadn't seen 'him.' I didn't see him or hear him that first day, and didn't hear him that second time either, till I mentioned where you was preaching. That's when I heard the bed. Like somebody had been laying in one place a long, long time—and when he heard what I said he turned over. No sound from him himself, just the screeching of the bed when he turned over.

"I had my back to the door, and I looked quick back over my shoulder. But nothing. Not another sound. Quiet, quiet. I kept my head that way, I don't know how long, but nothing. I looked back at her. She made 'tend she hadn't heard a thing. She even act like I hadn't even looked around. After we had been sitting there a while, not saying a thing, I asked her about the children.

"She told me the youngest boy and the girl was living in New York. Both married, both had a nice little family, and she heard from them all the time. Etienne, her oldest, was there with her. Everybody was doing just fine, just fine. Be sure to tell the people back home she was doing just fine, just fine.

"I didn't believe her. Not a bit. That's why I went back to the store to leave her some money. Both the man and his wife was behind the counter. Both watched me when I come in, like they knowed I was coming back. I took twenty dollars out my wallet and handed it to the woman. She didn't even wait for me to tell her what it was for.

" 'How come you didn't give it to her yourself?' she asked.

" 'She wouldn'ta took it,' I said.

"The old woman still looked at me. Didn't even nod her head. But she knowed what I was talking 'bout.

" 'When she come in the store I want you to—' But I didn't need to finish.

" 'I know,' the old woman said. 'She'll get it in grocery.'

" 'A little this time, a little next time, till it's all gone,' I said.

" 'I know how to do it,' the old lady said.

"Now both her and her husband just looked at me. They knowed why I was back.

" 'Well, I think I'll just go on up,' she said.

" 'Mama?' He stopped her.

"They looked at each other a long time, then she looked at me.

" 'What part Louisiana you say you from?' she asked.

" 'St. Raphael Parish.'

" 'Where's that?' she wanted to know.

" 'Between Lafayette and Baton Rouge, on the St. Charles River.'

" 'We know people from out that way,' she said. 'Honorable people.'

" 'I understand,' I said.

" 'Do you?'

" 'Yes.'

"She nodded her head. And looked back at her husband.

" 'Sure, Papa,' she said, and went upstairs.

" 'We knowed you was coming back,' he told me. 'Me and Mama talked 'bout it Tuesday night after you left here. We talked 'bout it today after she come over here and bought the food to cook. How was the food?'

" 'Good,' I said.

" 'Yes. We knowed you was coming back,' he said. 'Mama say we can trust you. Me, I don't know. Can I?'

" 'She's my friend,' I said. 'Her husband was my best friend.'

" 'Good,' he said. 'I'm sure glad to hear that. 'Cause you see he was the cause of it all.'

" 'Cause of what?' I asked.

" 'The trouble. What else?'

" 'What trouble?'

" 'I see,' he said. 'She didn't tell you 'bout the trouble. I bet you didn't get to see him either.'

" 'I didn't see nobody but her,' I said. 'But I think I heard somebody in that room.'

" 'A crypt,' he said.

" 'A crypt?'

" 'A crypt.'

" 'Why?'

" 'That's what I want you to tell me,' he said.

" 'Wait,' I said. 'Wait now.'

" 'Nobody else been able to tell me,' he said.

" 'Wait,' I said.

" 'No, you wait,' he said.

"He told me he had been knowing her 'bout fifteen years—ever since she first come to California. He remembered the day she got there, with nothing but her children and couple of beat-up old suitcases. That evening she come in his store to buy sausage and bread for sandwiches. His wife was behind the counter, and she invited her and the children to take supper with them that night. While she was there she told the old lady she needed work. She would do anything 'cause she didn't have any money. The old lady promised her credit at the store till she found a job. A week later she found housework for some white people. These people, Greeks, had a son called Mathias, studying law at a school there in Frisco. In the evenings he taught games and exercises at the YMCA, and every day he would take the children over there. Antoine and Justine would go with him, but Etienne had to work, help bring money in the house. He was the man of the house. The man of the house. She told it to him that day he left from here. She told it to him right there in front of me. When you didn't come out of Tut's house that day, she told him that till you did come back to them he was go'n be man of the house. She took him by the hand, looking straight in his face—a scared, confused little boy. I told her then it wasn't right. I told her he wasn't but a chap himself, and it wasn't right. I told her there'd be other men, and she oughtn't force this burden on him. But she didn't hear a word I said."

Chippo stopped and drank. Phillip who had raised his glass a couple of times was now holding the glass with both hands and staring over it at the floor. For a while he wasn't aware that Chippo had stopped talking. He had not been only listening to what Chippo was saying, but he was trying to picture in his mind things that Chippo was probably not telling him. His mind was constantly shifting from the house in San Francisco to the boy sitting beside him in the car today. Several times his mind had lingered on the boy too long, and he had missed some of the things that Chippo had said, but he never asked him to repeat anything. He probably wouldn't have been able to say anything even if he had tried. It was only when he realized that Chippo had stopped talking, that there had been silence a minute or two, that he looked at him again.

"What?" he said.

"The men."

"Go on."

"I don't like talking 'bout this."

"Go on."

"There was more than one, there was more than two."

"Go on."

"The storekeeper didn't know how many," Chippo said, looking closely at Phillip to let him know he found this unpleasant to talk about.

"Go on, Chippo," Phillip said.

"Never one too long. Two, three months, then he had to go. Be a long time when there wasn't one. Then another one—two, three months, then he was gone. The reason, none of them could be number one. She let them know that from the start. Number one was still in Louisiana. They could stay a while if they wanted to, then they had to get out.

"The last one wasn't a man, he was scum. Shooting pool was his trade, but he would do anything. From pushing dope to pimping to robbing the church—that was Quick George. They say he had been in that house no more than a month, when he turned from the mon to the daughter."

Chippo stopped again and looked at Phillip. "I'm telling you what the storekeeper said to me—nothing more. I wasn't there. I talked to nobody else. I'm telling it to you the way he told it to me. She wouldn't tell me nothing. He didn't want tell me nothing, and I didn't want tell you either. But I wanted to know what had happened, just like you want to know. I'm just telling it to you the way he told it to me. Lord knows I hate telling it. It's nothing somebody like talking 'bout."

Chippo waited for him to say something. He didn't. His jaws set tight, his eyes staring down at the floor, he waited. Chippo looked at him, drew in a deep breath, and exhaled harshly through his mouth.

"They heard Etienne and Antoine out there in the street fighting. His wife sent him out there to break it up. 'Fore he could reach them, Antoine had jumped up from the ground and was running. When he got closer he saw Etienne bleeding. He tried to get him back to the store, but Etienne got away from him and started running after his brother. Etienne running after Antoine, the storekeeper running after Etienne. Two blocks away from the pool hall where Quick George hung out, they heard the first shot. Two, three seconds later, another one. When they got there, Antoine was standing over Quick George with the .45 still pointed at his head. Etienne pushed his way through the crowd and tried to take the gun.

" 'It was me,' he said.

" 'It's too late now,' Antoine told him.

" 'No, it's not too late,' Etienne said. 'It was me. Everybody in here seen it was me. Didn't all y'all see it was me?'

" 'It's too late,' Antoine said. He went to the bar and told the bartender to call the law.

"According to the storekeeper, this what happened. The boys had come in the house a few minutes earlier and seen their sister laying on the bed crying. They didn't have to ask what had happened, they could see the dress, they could see the sheet. Etienne sat on the bed and took her in his arms, rocking and crying. Antoine went for the gun. (The storekeeper got all this from the young white lawyer who defended the boy later.) Antoine tried to push the gun on his brother. Etienne was the oldest, the man of the house, it was his job to do it.

" 'Go kill that dog,' Antoine told him.

" 'This for the law,' Etienne said.

" 'Law?' Antoine said. 'Law? There ain't no law when you rape a black girl. The raper was enticed. This the only law,' he said, pushing the gun on him.

" 'No,' Etienne said.

"Antoine tried to push the gun on him a third time. 'I say take it and go kill that dog.'

" 'No,' Etienne said. 'This for the law.'

" 'Then I'll do it for you,' Antoine said.

"They started fighting over the gun in the house. Etienne fighting to keep it there, Antoine fighting to use it. They fought in the house, out the door, in the street. That's how the storekeeper and his wife heard the noise. By the time he come out the store, Antoine had hit Etienne, and now Antoine was looking for Quick George.

"Quick George was shooting pool. Antoine shot as he come through the door. The first bullet missed. Maybe he was nervous, maybe he wanted to scare him 'fore he killed him. The bullet hit everything on that table but Quick George. The next one . . .

"She had been saving money in a jar. For what? For what? Days her and them children had gone hungry; years patches on top of patches on their clothes; a jar full of pennies, nickels, dimes, wrinkled dollar bills. She brought the jar to the storekeeper and asked him to take her to see the young lawyer that she had been working for. The lawyer told her to keep the money, let the expense fall on the state. He himself would work with the lawyer the state appointed —no charge at all."

Phillip was moving his body back and forth in the chair as someone might rock in a rocker. Not looking at Chippo, staring beyond him, rocking back and forth. Chippo stopped to look at him. But Phillip was unaware that Chippo was no longer speaking.

"Is that how he got here?" Chippo asked.

Phillip nodded his head, but he seemed only half aware that Chippo was talking to him.

"He musta stole that money," Chippo said. "I'm sure she—"

"Go on."

"I wouldn't believe it even if she told me herself. That woman loved you. It was him. Him. I know definitely it was him."

"Go on," Phillip said. "Go on."

"Man, you must believe that."

Phillip was not looking at him, he was waiting for him to go on.

Chippo, almost totally exasperated, watched him for a moment and started talking again.

"The boy got five years. The storekeeper said every week somebody went to see him. The young lawyer would take the family one time, the storekeeper or somebody else would take them the next time.

"Antoine and Justine was closer now than they had ever been. They would move away from Johanna and Etienne to whisper to each other. Antoine had nothing to say to his mama at all. If she asked him how he felt, he was all right. If she asked him if they was treating him good, it was always yes. If she asked him if he needed anything, it was always no. He had nothing to say to her. Nothing.

"Him and Etienne would talk. He had even forgiven Etienne for not taking the gun. But now he was the man, and he let Etienne know it. When he pulled that trigger, then he was the man. His sister, the way she looked at him, let him know that he was the man. Even Johanna. Even Etienne himself let him know that he was the man now.

"Justine stayed at the house with Johanna and Etienne till Antoine got out. Then both of them left. The last time anybody saw them was five, six years ago. They don't write to their mon or their brother. They write to the young lawyer who defended Antoine in court, and he tells Johanna 'bout them.

"After Antoine and Justine left, the people saw less and less of Johanna and Etienne. Johanna sometime, but Etienne hardly ever. One day the old lady, the storekeeper's wife, went over there and asked her about him.

" 'In there,' she said, nodding toward the room. Nothing else. Not another word. 'In there.'

"The same thing happened the second time, the third time. If the old lady stayed there long enough, she might hear him come out the room and go in the kitchen to eat. Always by himself. They didn't even eat together any more. The old lady had gone there when Johanna was eating, and he would be in his room. If he ate while she was there, she would hear him washing his plate quiet quiet, using little water as he could, then back to his room. One time when he was sick, the old lady made Johanna let her in there to see him. In the room, a narrow bunk, a little chest of drawers, nails against the wall to hang his clothes—that was all. A crypt.

"Why he went in there? Who knows? Did Johanna make him go in there? Did he go in on his own? Who knows for sure? I believe he went in there out of guilt. He wasn't the man of the house no more, and he didn't want act like he was.

"At night he went out walking. The people saw him. Then back to the house—to the room—laying there woke, listening, waiting. Waiting. Waiting. Waiting for what? Another chance? He had failed his sister. What was he waiting for—to defend mama? That's why he lay there waiting? What other reason?

"Then I knocked . . ."

Chippo stopped. He was tired. He had drunk the last of the whiskey in his glass. Now he rolled the empty glass round in the palms of both hands while he stared down at the heater.

"That's what the storekeeper told me," he said, looking at Phillip. "Exactly how he told it to me. After he was through he told me never repeat this where it might hurt her. Well, I'm glad now I told you. I can go to Reno now and see the old people, and I don't have to feel guilty 'bout holding nothing from them. I feel good about it. Yes. Like somebody done gone to confession."

Phillip looked at him. "That's how you feel?"

"Exactly," Chippo said.

Phillip nodded his head. "I see," he said. "I see. It musta been a heavy burden to carry, Chippo."

11

For a long time now they were quiet. Chippo was tired, drained of all physical strength, but his mind relieved. Relieved of a burden, as he had said, as one's mind is relieved after going to confession. The body was still tired though, from wandering, gambling through the evening and the night, and especially from talking about something that he didn't find pleasant. He pulled out an old brass-covered watch to check the time. It was five minutes to two.

"I ought to be going," Phillip said.

He was just as tired as Chippo. But where Chippo's mind had been relieved of a burden by talking about it, Phillip now felt a heavier burden by hearing it.

"You going?" Chippo asked him.

"Before it get any later. We have to talk again."

"Talk about what, man?"

Phillip shook his head. "I don't know. But we have to talk again."

"Why don't you stay here tonight and rest?"

"Rest?" Phillip said. His forehead wrinkled as if the word was foreign to him. "Rest?"

"You can use some rest."

"Yes, I can use some rest."

"Then stay here," Chippo said. "Nothing that can't wait till tomorrow."

"This can't wait, Chippo," Phillip said.

"It waited this long."

"It's waited too long, Chippo," Phillip said, and looked at him. "Don't you see? It's waited too long."

"And you go'n make it up tonight?"

"You got to start sometime."

Chippo leaned over and got the bottle and poured just a little whiskey into his glass.

"What's been done been done, man," he said, after he had drunk. "A terrible thing happened, yes; but you can't do a thing 'bout it. My honest opinion—forget it."

Phillip laughed. It was not a time to laugh. Chippo watched him. He laughed again, a deep, strange chest laugh.

"You know how hard I been trying to forget it?" he asked Chippo. Chippo didn't answer him. "I went to religion to forget it. I prayed and prayed and prayed to forget it. I tried to wipe out everything in my past, make my mind blank, start all over. I thought the good work I was doing with the church, with the people, would make up for all the things I had done in the past. Till one day I looked cross my living room. . . . Forget it? If it was that easy, you think I'd be sitting here with you now?" he asked, and shook his head. "But from the moment I saw him in that house—I fell, Chippo. I fell. When I saw him in that room my legs buckled, and I fell. When I got up—I didn't tell them I fell because I recognized my son in the house."

"Wait," Chippo said.

Phillip told him about the party, and how Etienne happened to be there.

"I laid on that floor, Chippo, and listened to Octave Bacheron telling the people I fell because I was tired. Why, Chippo? Why? When will we break that bond? When will we stand up and tell our people the truth? When will we make our legs go to our sons and make our arms protect our sons? When, Chippo? When?"

Phillip searched Chippo's face for the answer, but Chippo couldn't think of anything to say.

"I met a young man tonight, a young vet'ran, wearing all his Army green. A grenade scar on his face. Been's close to death as you can get. Angry. Angry. Angry. He told me the whole civil rights movement ain't done a thing. Ain't done a thing, 'cause him and his father and me and my boy ain't no closer than we ever was. And he's right, Chippo. We ain't no closer than we ever was." Phillip took a deep breath and stood up. He was very tired. He held on to the back of the chair while he looked down at Chippo. "I was telling my boy today what keep us apart is a paralysis we inherited from slavery. Paralysis kept me on that bed that day he knocked on that door. Paralysis kept me on that floor Saturday when I shoulda got up and told the people who he was. I thought fifteen years ago when I found religion I had overthrown my paralysis. But it's still there, Chippo. How do you get rid of it? How do you shake it off?"

Chippo didn't know how to answer him. Phillip started toward the sofa to get his hat and coat but stopped when he heard a car door slam in front of the house. Chippo went to the door to see who was out there. Alma stood before him in a long black overcoat and a scarf tied on her head. Behind her were Shepherd and Beverly.

"Mr. Chippo," Alma spoke softly.

Chippo nodded his head. He could tell by her quiet, strained voice, by her slightly swollen face, that she had been crying. He looked back at Shepherd as if to ask him what had happened, but before Shepherd could answer he moved to let them come in. Phillip stood near the couch watching them. Alma could speak his name, but she was unable to go on. Shepherd came round her and motioned for Phillip to sit down. Phillip moved back to the sofa, feeling for it with his hand but never taking his eyes off Shepherd's face. After he had sat down, Shepherd stood over him. Phillip could see in his face that he didn't want to say it either, what both of them had come there to tell him.

"Today at three o'clock, Alcee Lejean saw him standing on that trestle over Big Man Bayou. Late tonight"—Shepherd had to check his voice a moment—"Nolan and his deputies pulled him out of the water."

Phillip started shaking his head. "That's not so, that's not so, that's not so," he said. "God knows, that's not so."

Alma came to the sofa to sit beside him, but he didn't see her. He was still looking up at Shepherd.

"I was just coming back home to talk to him," Phillip said. "Chippo's my witness there. Chippo just told me his name. I was coming back home to talk to him. Tell him, Chippo."

Chippo, still over by the door, did not answer. Phillip was still watching Shepherd, his face trembling. Alma laid her hand on his arm, but he didn't feel it.

"I don't believe it," Phillip said to Shepherd. "I don't believe it. Why you tell me this? Bring me this kind of news?"

Alma squeezed his arm, but he didn't feel it.

"Why, boy?" he asked Shepherd.

"Nobody like to bear this kind of news, Reverend," Shepherd said. "But we talked about this last night. We saw it coming, Reverend."

"I didn't see it coming," Phillip said.

"Robert was your son, Reverend Martin."

"Etienne," Phillip corrected him. "Not Robert. Not X. Etienne. Etienne Martin. And Antoine Martin, and Justine Martin. That's why I come to Baton Rouge tonight. Now you bring me that kind of news?"

"I'm sorry," Shepherd said.

Phillip started to say something else, but instead lowered his head. Shepherd standing over him could see his shoulders begin to shake as his head went lower and lower to his chest. Alma tried comforting him, but as soon as he felt her hand, he wiped his eyes and reached for his hat and coat. He adjusted his hat well on his head, then as he stood up to put on the coat he suddenly stopped as if he had just remembered something.

"Go where?" he said to himself. "Go to what? To what?" He looked at Chippo. "I had forgot. I had forgot. They took the leadership from me today. They say I'm not fit no more. And I had forgot all about that."

"They can't do that," Chippo said.

"They did it already," Phillip said, and looked at Alma sitting on the sofa. "They say I'm not fit no more."

"Who suppose to lead?" Chippo asked.

"Jonathan," Phillip said, looking down at Alma, who sat on the sofa with her hands clasped together and her head bowed. "My young punk assistant."

"Your assistant?" Chippo asked. "Who can he lead?"

"That's who they want," Phillip said. "That's who all of them want. Well, they can have him."

He went to the heater and got the bottle and poured up a good shot, drank it down fast, then poured up another one. He looked at Alma, who had stood up and was buttoning her coat.

"Where you think you going?" he asked her.

"I'm going home with you."

"Who say I'm going home?"

He drank half the whiskey in the glass and looked back at her.

"I met an old gal tonight," he said. He was drunk now, and he didn't care who knew it. "Hadn't seen her in fifteen years. Think I'll go pay her a little visit."

Alma looked at him a moment, then finished buttoning up the overcoat.

"If that's what you need to do," she said.

"That's what I'm going to do," he told her.

"I'll go back with Shepherd and Beverly," Alma said. "I'll be home when you get there."

"So I'm fit, now, huh?" he said to her. "After he kill himself I'm fit again, huh?"

"I never said you wasn't fit," Alma said. "I just said they wasn't go'n stand for you to treat them the way you treat me."

"Well, nobody need to stand for nothing I do no more," Phillip said, and finished off his drink. He set the bottle and the glass back down on the floor.

"Where you think you going?" Chippo asked him.

"Adeline Toussaint told me to drop by," Phillip said, and grinned drunkenly at him. "You remember her, don't you? Pretty yellow woman. Good snatch. Never cared about a damn thing. You remember her, Chippo. You got some of that stuff too, didn't you?"

"You not going to that whore," Chippo said. "Not out of my house."

"No?" Phillip said.

"No," Chippo said.

"Let him go, Mr. Chippo," Alma said. "He's probably got lot of them he go to."

Phillip looked at her. "No," he said. "I used to have lot of whores. Once I had more whores than Carter got liver pills. But I ain't slept with another woman but you the last fifteen years. Till tonight."

He started toward the door. Chippo moved in his way.

"You think I'm go'n let you go to that whore?"

"You go'n stop me?" Phillip asked him.

"I'm go'n try," Chippo said.

"Chippo, you never could stand up to this before," Phillip said, showing him a fist about the size of an eight-ounce boxing glove. "What make you think you can stand up to it now?"

"Me and that boy there can do it," Chippo said.

"You in this too, Shepherd?" Phillip asked him.

Shepherd had taken one look at Phillip's big fist. The last thing he wanted was to have anything to do with it. But his woman was there, and he had no other choice.

"I think he's right," he said weakly.

Phillip grunted and started round Chippo. Chippo got to the door before he did.

"I got grief in me, Chippo," Phillip told him. "I got grief in me, and I got fury in me."

"And that whore can change all that?"

"I'm warning you, Chippo," Phillip said. "Move out my way."

"Move out his way, Mr. Chippo," Alma said. "Move out his way. Let him go to his whore."

Chippo didn't move. And he didn't see the punch coming either. It landed on his left jaw and he went down. He was down, but he was not out, and as Phillip tried stepping over him, Chippo grabbed one of his legs and pulled him back in the room. Halfway cross the room Phillip jerked his leg free and started back for the door. Shepherd was there this time, his hands up, palms out toward Phillip.

"Now, take it easy, Reverend," he said. "He's right. Take it easy, take it easy."

"Get out the way, boy," Phillip said.

"Take it easy, Reverend."

"Get out my way, boy."

"Take it easy, Reverend."

Phillip swung. Shepherd blocked it neatly. But his arm felt as if someone had hit him with a baseball bat. Phillip drew back to hit him again, but Chippo was up now, and grabbed his arm and swung him cross the room. Phillip hit the sofa and sprung back up as quickly as if he had landed on a trampoline. Now he stood wide-legged, his two big fists poised. He didn't care about going through that door any more. All he wanted now was a fight.

"Stop it," Alma screamed at Chippo. "Stop it." She ran up to him and tried to pull him away from the door. "Let him go," she said. "Let him go. Let him go to all his women. Let him go."

Chippo pushed her to the side. He pushed her a little too hard and she fell. Beverly, who had been standing with her back to the wall, helped her up and led her to the next room, crying.

Shepherd and Chippo were still blocking the door, watching Phillip. If he came on them they would grab him on either side. They watched him standing there breathing hard, his two big fists poised and shaking. No one moved, no one would dare move, but they were still watching one another.

Then suddenly he turned from them and started looking round the room. He was looking for something to hit, something to break. But there was nothing near him. The walls were too far for him to reach. The chairs were too far away, the bottle, the glass were all out of his reach. He jerked his head back to face Shepherd and Chippo again. They were still watching him, still ready for him if he came on them. But after a while, they saw his eyes go slowly toward the floor. His breathing became more normal, and his hands went to his side. He moved back to the sofa and sat down, his head hanging almost to his chest.

Chippo took in a deep breath and went over to the heater, leaving Shepherd alone at the door.

"I know how you must feel, man," he said after a while.

"No, you don't," Phillip said.

"I know, man," Chippo said.

"Nobody know how this nigger feels," Phillip said gazing down at the floor, his big arms hanging down between his legs the way a defeated fighter's arms would hang. "You work, you work—what good it do? You bust your ass—what good it do? Man and God, both in one day, tell you go to hell, go fuck yourself."

"Don't, man," Chippo said, and looked toward the other room where the women were.

Phillip was quiet. Chippo watched him sitting there with his head down and his arms hanging between his legs. Over at the door, Shepherd was still rubbing his arm where Phillip had hit him.

"It's over with," Phillip said.

"No, man," Chippo said.

"It's over with, and I'm glad," Phillip said. "I don't have to lie and beg and plead with them no more. Let them do what they want."

"And what happen then?" Chippo asked.

"I don't care."

"You do care, man," Chippo said. "That's for somebody like me to say—'I don't care.' That's for the rest of them no-'count niggers on East Boulevard to say—'I don't care.' Not for you, man. Hanh, Shepherd?"

"No," Shepherd said from the door.

"Somebody got to care, man," Chippo said to Phillip. "Somebody got to keep on caring. He go'n get hurt caring, but he can't never stop. I'm right or I'm wrong there, Shepherd?" Chippo asked, without looking at Shepherd.

"You right," Shepherd said.

"You can't stop, man," Chippo said to Phillip. "We need you out there too much. Just like you see me—this old ugly half-blind nigger—I need you out there. I need somebody to look up to. There ain't nobody else left out there to look up to. You, I look up to. Me, plenty more like me, we look up to you. I'm right or I'm wrong there, Shepherd?"

"You right, Chippo," Shepherd said. He rubbed his arm. He wondered if it was broken.

Phillip raised his head and looked at Chippo standing at the heater.

"It's over with, Chippo," he said. "It's over with. They beat me down today. They caught me staggering, and they jecked the rug from under my feet."

"You can get up man. Hanh, Shepherd?"

"Sure."

"Even Him," Phillip went on, as if he hadn't heard either Shepherd or Chippo. "How come He let this happen? How come He stood by me all these years, but not today? I've walked through mobs after mobs. Traveled every dark muddy road in this state. 'Cause I knowed He was there with me. Why He give me all that strength, that courage to do all them other things, and when I asked Him for my boy—" He stopped. His mouth trembled. Tears came into his eyes. "Why didn't He hear me, Chippo? What is it, Chippo? Why won't He let this poor black man reach his son? Was that so hard to do? Was that asking Him for too much? Well, Chippo?"

Chippo shrugged his shoulders. "I don't understand His ways, man. They say what He do He do for the best."

"To let my boy die like that, that's for the best? That's what you saying, Chippo?"

Chippo didn't answer.

"Them today," Phillip went on, "Mills, Aaron, Peter—why couldn't they understand? Why couldn't they see that all this black man wanted was to touch his son? What's so hard about that, Chippo? Tell me, what's so hard about that?"

Chippo knew he had no more to offer than what he had already said, so he did not try to answer. Phillip looked at Shepherd at the door holding his arm.

"Well, boy?"

"I don't know the answer either, Reverend," Shepherd said.

"You don't know the answer, and you got in my way?" Phillip asked him. "When you block a man from doing one thing, you ought to have something better to offer him. Well?"

Shepherd shook his head. He wondered if his arm was broken.

"You teach school, don't you?" Phillip asked him.

"I teach school."

"And how you answer the children?"

"Depends on the question, Reverend."

"You done lost faith, boy," Phillip said. "You done lost it all? How you tell them that?"

"You don't," Chippo said.

"How you tell them that, boy?" Phillip asked Shepherd, without looking at Chippo. "How you tell them that?"

"I don't know, Reverend."

"Don't you have faith in anything, boy?"

"Not too much," Shepherd said, looking straight at him.

Phillip nodded his head. "That's a good way to be, boy. The only way to be. That way you never get hurt."

"That's not a good way to be," Chippo said. "You got to have faith in something. Me, I have faith in you."

"You damn fool, Chippo," Phillip said. "Be like that boy there. Don't put no faith in nothing. Not in God. Not in work. Not in love. In nothing. Put it in the bottle. That's a good place to put your faith, huh, boy? The bottle?"

Shepherd looked at him, but he didn't say anything. He wished he had never stood before that door.

In the other room Alma lay down across the bed, and Beverly sat on the bed beside her listening to the men in the front room. She was trying to think of something that she might be able to go in there and say. She looked back at Alma and asked her if she was all right. Alma nodded her head. Beverly touched her on the shoulder and left the room.

When she came into the front room, the men got quiet. She stood back a moment looking at all of them, then she went to the sofa and sat down close to Phillip. For a moment all she did was look at him. Then she took one of his big hands and began caressing the knuckles, gently, gently. The men watched her, but they stayed quiet.

"You have to go back," she said.

Phillip pulled his hand free.

"Back to what?" he asked her.

"To St. Adrienne," she said quietly as she looked up at him. "To your wife, your children, your church. Even to the ones back there who don't have faith in anything," she said, and looked round at Shepherd.

"I don't have none either," Phillip said.

"I don't believe that," she said to him. "You've been hurt. You've been hurt bad. But a man like you can't lose faith that easily."

"You can lose it that easily," he said. "After you work and work and work, and everything fall apart all at the same time, you can lose it that easily."

She shook her head. "You wanted too much, Reverend. You wanted too much from man, from God. Too much all at one time. It don't work that way."

Phillip studied her closely a moment, then he sat back in the sofa. Shepherd and Chippo watched both of them.

"Do you know me?" Phillip asked Beverly.

"Reverend Phillip J. Martin," Beverly said.

"Did you know me before I was Reverend Phillip J. Martin?"

"No," she said.

"I didn't think you did," he said, and looked at her a while before going on. "I was an animal before I was Reverend Phillip J. Martin. I was an animal. He changed me to a man. He straightened my back. He raised my head. He gave me feelings, compassion, made me responsible for my fellow man. My back wasn't straightened before he straightened it. My eyes stayed on the ground. I took everything I could from my fellow man, and I didn't give him nothing back.

"The last fifteen years I've gived, and gived, and gived to my fellow man. I've taken my fellow man by the hand and led him the way you lead a small child: led him to that courthouse, led him to the stores, led him to that bus station. I've felt my fellow man tremble in my hands the way you feel voltage in a 'lectric wire. I've seen four hundred years of fear in his eyes when I asked him to sit on a bench beside me, or to have a drink of water from a fountain. But I asked nobody to do a thing till I had done it first. I was ready to get the first blow, what I've received many many times. But I kept going, kept going. 'Cause of Him. 'Cause of Him. 'Cause of Him I've been running after my son. I never woulda done it if it wasn't for Him. I woulda looked at my son going by the house, and I woulda forgotten him—if it wasn't for Him. But He changed me, and I can't forget my son. I can't forget my son, young lady. I can't ignore my son no more. That's why I say He owed me my son. Once He made me a human being He owed me my son."

Beverly looked at him and smiled. She admired this big man sitting beside her.

"He's paid you," she said. "Rewarded you for your work many times. Can't you see how many times He's rewarded you?"

She waited for him to answer her. He looked at her as if he didn't know what she was talking about.

"The ones you led to that courthouse, to that fountain, don't tremble any more when they lean over to get a drink of water. Isn't that payment enough?"

"They're the same ones who told me to go to hell today," Phillip said.

"Who told you that?" Beverly asked. "How many? Five? Six? And I'm sure they don't mean it. And even if they did, how about all the rest? There're many more people who walk up to that courthouse today without trembling. I go up there today without trembling. Shepherd go up there today without trembling. I take my class there, and they walk all through that courthouse without trembling. Your son Patrick is in my class. He's one of the proudest little boys you'll ever meet. Why? Because Daddy made all this possible. Isn't that payment enough, Reverend Martin?"

"I'm talking about my son," he said.

"Patrick is your son too, isn't he? Isn't Patrick your son, Reverend Martin?"

He didn't answer her. He didn't know how to answer her. He didn't like the way she was turning things around.

"You wanted the past changed, Reverend Martin," she told him. "Even He can't do that. So that leaves nothing but the future. We work toward the future. To keep Patrick from going to that trestle. One day I'll have a son, and what we do tomorrow might keep him from going to that trestle. That's all we can ever hope for, isn't it, Reverend Martin? That's all we work for, isn't it?"

He didn't answer her. She picked up his hand again.

"Your hands are so big," she said. "So strong. The hands of a fighter. These hands belong to a fighter."

She laid his hand back on his leg and stood up.

"You ought to go in there to her," she said. She turned to Shepherd. "You ready to go?"

"Sure."

Beverly went into the other room to tell Alma that she was leaving. When she came back out she went over to the sofa and kissed Phillip on the side of the face.

"You won't let us down, will you?"

He looked at her but didn't answer her. She turned for the door. Shepherd shook hands with Chippo, nodded to Phillip, and followed her out of the room. Chippo went as far as the door with them and then came back to the heater. He stood with his back to it and looked at Phillip.

"They married?"

"No," Phillip said.

"I'll give him a month."

"You think so?" Phillip asked.

"Sure's my name's Erin Simon," Chippo said.

Both of them could hear the springs as Alma turned over on the bed in the other room.

"I think I might go for a little walk," Chippo said.

"This time of morning?" Phillip asked him.

"I'm a rover," Chippo said. "Don't matter to me what time it is."

He came to the sofa to get his hat and coat.

"Just push the door if y'all leave," he said.

"When you coming home, Chippo?" Phillip asked him.

"I'll come in later today," Chippo said, and went out.

Phillip sat there watching the door a long time after Chippo had gone. Finally he pushed himself up and went into the other room.

"Everybody's gone?" Alma asked him.

"Yes, everybody's gone."

He lay down on the bed beside her. And she moved up close against him.

"I'm lost, Alma. I'm lost."

"Shhh," she said. "Shhh. Shhh. We just go'n have to start again."

A Note on the Type

The text of this book was set in Caledonia, a Linotype face designed by W. A. Dwiggins. It belongs to the family of printing types called "modern face" by printers—a term used to mark the change in style of type letters that occurred about 1800. Caledonia borders on the general design of Scotch Modern, but is more freely drawn than that letter.

Composed by Maryland Linotype Composition Company, Inc., Baltimore, Maryland. Printed and bound by The Haddon Craftsmen, Inc., Scranton, Pennsylvania. Typography and binding design by Karolina Harris.